where they come from
where they hide

where they come from
where they hide

Phillip Gardner

LITERARY PRESS
LAMAR UNIVERSITY

ISBN: 978-1-942956-62-4
Library of Congress Control Number: 2019940934

Lamar University Literary Press
Beaumont, Texas

Once again for Tressa

Books from Lamar University Literary Press include

Robert Bonazzi, *Awakened by Surprise*
David Bowles, *Flower, Song, Dance: Aztec and Mayan Poetry*
David Bowles, *Border Lore: Folktales and Legends of South Texas*
Jerry Bradley, *Crownfeathers and Effigies*
Jerry Bradley and Ulf Kirchdorfer, editors, *The Great American Wise Ass Poetry Anthology*
Matthew Brennan, *One Life*
Mark Busby, *Through Our Times*
Kevin K. Casey, *Four-Peace*
Stan Crawford, *Resisting Gravity*
Terry Dalrymple, *Love Stories (Sort Of)*
Terry Dalrymple, editor, *Texas Weather: An Anthology of Poetry, Short Fiction, and Nonfiction*
Chip Dameron, *Waiting for an Etcher*
William Virgil Davis, *The Bones Poems*
Jeffrey DeLotto, *Voices Writ in Sand*
Jeffrey DeLotto, *A Caddo's Way*
Chris Ellery, *Elder Tree*
Ted Estess, *Fishing Spirit Lake*
Ken Hada, *Margaritas and Redfish*
Britt Haraway, *Early Men*
Katherine Hoerth, *Goddess Wears Cowboy Boots*
Lynn Hoggard, *Motherland, Stories and Poems from Louisiana*
Gretchen Johnson, *The Joy of Deception*
Gretchen Johnson, *A Trip Through Downer, Minnesota*
Tom Mack and Andrew Geyer, editors, *A Shared Voice*
Janet McCann, *The Crone at the Casino*
Laurence Musgrove, *Local Bird*
Laurence Musgrove, *One Kind of Recording, Aphorisms*
Dave Oliphant, *The Pilgrimage, Selected Poems: 1962-2012*
Moumin Quazi, *Migratory Words*
Harold Raley, *Louisiana Rogue*
Harold Raley, *Lost River Anthology*
Carol Coffee Reposa, *Underground Musicians*
Jim Sanderson, *Trashy Behavior*
Jim Sanderson, *Sanderson's Fiction Writing Manual*
Jan Seale, *Appearances*
Jan Seale, *The Parkinson Poems*
Jan Seale, *Ordinary Charms*
Steven Schroeder, *What's Love Got to Do With It?*
Melvin Sterne, *The Number You Have Reached*
Gary Swaim, *Quixotic Notions*
Loretta Diane Walker, *Desert Light*
John Wegner, *Love is Not a Dirty Word*
Robert Wexelblatt, *The Artist Wears Rough Clothing*
Dan Williams, *Past Purgatory, A Distant Paradise*

For information on these and other books, go to www.lamar.edu/literarypress

Acknowledgments

Thanks to the editors and staff at the following, where versions of these stories first appeared:

Apalachee Review
Emrys Journal
Hayden's Ferry Review
Jasper
Louisiana Literature
New Delta Review
North American Review
Rainbow Curve
r.k.v.r.y. Quarterly
storySouth

I owe decades of gratitude to these teachers, colleagues and writers: Doris Becton, Jill Carraway, Dick Croy, Debra Daniel, Tom Mack, Nancy and David McCallister, Robert Parham, Lynn Kostoff, Ron Rash, George Singleton and Jon Tuttle.

Other Books by Phillip Gardner

Someone To Crawl Back To
somebody wants somebody dead
Available Light
The Future Never Lasts

CONTENTS

These stories are meant to be read in order.

Vapor

"You're the guy in the turtleneck."

After I've been introduced to people for the third or fourth time, that's what they say. These introductions are a kind of tag-team event, which I will explain. Although it's not likely that you'll remember, you need to know who I am, a little something about me.

Think of me as a sort of vapor, you know, a presence without substance. No, that's not it. I don't really have what you might call excellent social or communication skills. What I have is a face that's like a blank screen, really. My facelessness has become my trademark: I'm the man in the turtleneck with the empty face—but you can call me *Vapor*. Actually, when I say it like that, it sounds like the name of a hot sports car or a rock star, you know, Prince, Sting, Vapor.

Sometimes when I'm out having a drink, I'll look around and imagine that I *am* Vapor, that mysterious guy at the bar in the turtleneck with the face nobody can remember. Pretending I'm incognito is unnecessary, but the next best thing to being the man of a thousand faces is being the man with no face at all. As you will come to know.

At some time, you've probably been approached by a stranger who says, "You're so-and-so, aren't you?" Or another who says, "You probably hear this all the time, but you really do look like so-and-so." Not me. Me, I take a barstool at The Paradise Lounge, order a drink, and five minutes later Tami, the bartender, says, "How's it hangin', stranger?" Again. I'll hold up my bourbon, and she'll say, "Oh, yeah, you're the guy in the turtleneck." I lower my voice a couple of octaves and whisper, "Vapor's the name." She doesn't hear me.

When our class went on fieldtrips as kids, I was the one responsible for the teacher's counting heads and then doing the math again.

I've never had many friends, which may account for my less than par social skills. Or it could be the other way around. Anyway, remember what I just said, that word "par," it really turns out to be clever later on when I get into the story, one I call "Chainsaw Putt-Putt."

11

What I lack in social graces, social adjustment, I've made up for in imagination. I have what my school psychologist, Mr. Spring, called a "rich interior life." He said I needed to find some healthy, constructive outlet. Which I have done. If he remembered me, which he doesn't, he'd be proud.

You see, I took his advice, turning a disadvantage into an advantage. Instead of becoming a wallflower who spent his life alone consuming popcorn and beer in front of a television and slowly swelling like a blowfish, I began to live the *Vapor* life.

Use what you've got, Mr. Spring told me.

As you might guess, I wasn't very popular in school. Never invited to parties, never went to the prom, etcetera. But when I finally began taking my shrink's advice, things changed. After I graduated, I attended my high school's Junior-Senior dance five years in a row. I introduced myself to Mr. Spring, the psychologist, every year. I even danced with his wife a couple of times.

In my late twenties, Vapor's social life orbited around the summer and winter solstices, the months of June and December. In June there were the wedding receptions, in December, the Christmas parties. I'd just show up, introduce myself to someone as a relative or fellow employee and hang around until he or she tired of sustaining a conversation, since that's not one of my strong suits, whereupon I'd be passed off to someone else, eating and drinking and making merry all the while. I was like one of those guys at rock concerts who floats above the mosh pit.

I know what you're thinking. Not that I read minds, but I do have a rich interior life. What you're thinking is, I believe I've met that guy before, maybe at so-and-so's wedding or at last year's company Christmas party. This turtleneck stuff is starting to sound familiar, that's what you're thinking.

Another of my favorite events is the annual Redneck Party in my hometown of Darlington, which is a town too tough to tame if you're really hip to NASCAR lingo. Every Labor Day weekend, a.k.a. the Southern 500 race weekend, a group of my neighbors puts on a party, something like a block party, only bigger. I'm told they send out invitations, but I always just crashed it. I don't think anybody asks to see invitations or that anybody counts heads. Besides, what did I have to worry about? Someone would say, "Hey, I think that guy's crashing our party," and the other might say, "What does he look like?" And the first would say, "How the hell do I know?" And I would be standing next to the beer keg, nodding a big uh-huh.

You see, I don't want you to think that I was an unhappy guy. I have a good job at the Darlington Flower Shoppe, which is perfect for a guy like me. But I *was* what you might call a lonely guy. Those aren't the same. If I had a gift for gab, I'd explain the difference. What I *can* say is the world is a very strange place when you can see out but nobody can see in. It's like the opposite of being a blind man, to have an invisible face. I'm no good at explaining. Let me put it like this: If you are a human being with a heart, you're gonna have one or two encounters that your heart always remembers. Here's mine.

It was at the Redneck Party that I saw her, my Rosiland Mammond. I mean saw her again. After high school graduation, she went away to college and became an actress and then a drama teacher in Florence, ten miles away. I'd see her picture in the paper once in a while, and I'd attend performances when she was in Little Theater productions. Okay, she had been nice to me in high school or so I thought, given my limited social skills. Anyway, she knew who I was.

You probably won't think it's very romantic, I mean it took place in the high school cafeteria for Pete's sake, in front of three hundred kids, their faces forming a landscape of pimple volcanoes, each slopping greasy spaghetti into their traps, but I don't care what you think because my heart has this snapshot of Rosiland Mammon—which is the girl's name in case you haven't figured it out—of Rosiland, with her hands framing my cheeks, see, and she's standing over me at the lunch table, and she's studying my face, I mean really. She says to me in the most sincere and honest voice—talk about social skills—she says, "How do you *do* that? What kind of power does it take to empty your face of all expression?"

And now half the lunchroom is looking on. And then she does the thing that I'll carry to my grave. She says, "Can I touch it?" and if you're a guy, you can guess what happened next and if you're not, I can't tell you in a socially acceptable way. And I say, "Uh-huh." Then she closes her eyes like a blind person and she touches my face, I mean all over, with her eyes closed. And tears start to bead out and I'm—well, I'm making no expression at all, of course. Finally, she says, "Thank you," in this real breathy voice, like she just discovered the wonderland of O, and then turns and walks out, to a standing ovation. All afternoon kids were talking about it, and I heard a few of them ask, "Who was that guy?" And the other says, "Don't know. Never seen him before."

So, I'm standing beside one of the beer kegs at the Redneck Party in Darlington, the town that's too tough to tame, and I see Rosiland Mammon, who's with some beefy, blockhead guy with a fifty-dollar haircut—I know what I'm talking about here—and wearing five-hundred dollars' worth of Harley leather. I really, really hate that sort, you know, the country club kind who wants to play bad-boy phony-fart biker-thug on weekends? That type. Anyway, what I see is Rosiland Mammon and this puffy banker biker who's sort of bearing down on her, holding his Budweiser up like he's gonna hit her with it, and shaking his Polo cologned jaws in her face like a rabid Saint Bernard.

And she's got tears in her eyes.

It came to me like a revelation at a redneck party. I wanted to pull the plug on the CD player, stand on the keg and shout, "Hey, y'all, watch *this*!" Then I'd mutilate Mr. G.Q. Cycleboy.

At that second, Rosiland Mammon slowly lifted these pleading eyes—and she looked at *me*, with this expression from a silent movie all over her face and then Mr. Phony-Frat Fart-Faced Biker-Boy has her by the arm and drags her away, and they disappear into the crowd.

Suddenly the old feeling came back. All my vapor evaporated. I was my old faceless self again. A kid standing alone. At once, this loneliness like a huge black vat of history starts rising around me and pretty soon I'm treading water in it, and I'm getting this old film footage that my heart has tried to X, like my childhood, and how my mom, and that time playing snake when blah, blah, blah, and then I'm thinking of when I tried to, you know, put an end to it all by cutting off my faceless head with a chainsaw. But mostly I'm thinking about that silent movie look on Rosiland Mammon's face, and the gnawing feeling in my gut that would go away once I'd wasted Mr. Two-wheel Tubby-Boy.

I probably should have left out that part, you know, the part that now I have to tell you about because when the words start coming out—. It really isn't the story I'm trying to tell you, but once you've mentioned the two words in the same sentence—those would be suicide and chainsaw—. So here's the short version, so I can get on with it, which maybe isn't such a bad idea because the chainsaw figures in the story. Par for the course.

I'd been playing that Prince song *1999* for maybe three or four hours, and yes, I'd been drinking and it was closing in on midnight. This was New Year's Eve 1999. Not everybody believes in those end-of-the-world scenarios, but I happen to be one who does. When you've seen the things I saw as a kid. My father exploding into tiny red flecks. Anyway,

I'm thinking Y-2K, which may sound funny to you now, but you never heard Vincent Howle's visionary Armageddon sermon and all the rest, so I'm thinking, What if this *is* the end of time? What is the one thing I have to do, you know, if you can put yourself in the mind of a guy who's looking at the clock as if it's The Final Countdown?

So I call her number, and when she answers—remember this is Rosiland Mammon on the other end of the line and it's almost midnight on New Year's Eve 1999—it's like a miracle. The thing you dream about and wait for your whole life, and wham! There she is, her voice on the other end of the line. We talk a little, but I don't know what I said, something really socially inept you can be sure, and then as the long hand nears twelve, I do the one thing I have to do. I ask her if she'd like to go out with me sometime, and she says in a way that I still think had a little bit of sadness in it, at least a touch, she says that she's seeing somebody. And then there's this long pause—where I should have been backing out of the conversation gracefully, for both our sakes—but the next thing I know, I'm outside in the garage listening to the neighbors' fireworks and making sure the oil-fuel mixture is right for the chainsaw. End of story.

The real story concerns what came about after the Redneck party. Me and Mr. Black Harley Chaps with the boots and the sinister decal on the fancy as hell black trailer that he transports his bike in because as you know it's all show. The guy's heart lives on the stock exchange. And what happens is, I start following him around, I mean up close and personal.

Finding him was easy. There's this NASCAR-theme restaurant in Florence called Red Meat Rally where his type hangs out. That part was a cinch. Really all of it was a cinch, including like I said, tailing him. It became a highly secret operation in the life of Vapor. I wore the black turtleneck for about a week on maybe fifteen occasions. I sat beside him at bars and across from him at restaurants, until one day in Charleston he looked up as we stood side by side in a Chinese buffet line, and I watched him having a déjà vu moment. So I changed to the white turtleneck, then the red one.

I spent my days off from the Darlington Flower Shoppe following him back and forth across South Carolina, from Rock Hill, to Columbia, to Spartanburg, to Charleston, to Myrtle Beach. Unless you ever drove by and saw the signs and wondered who the owner was, you wouldn't know my guy owns all the King-Putt golf courses in the state. The king of King Putts, that's my guy.

15

Being a man with a rich interior life, I have to say that I spent most of those hours on the road thinking about slicing and dicing the King of Putts, not that I would ever do any of the things I thought about doing. But I liked thinking about doing them, and if you know the type of guy I'm talking about you'd enjoy thinking about them too. So here's a sampling. I'd chainsaw him at the elbows and knees. Then I'd superglue his fingers around the Harley's grips, elbows pointed skyward, and glue the bottom of his boots, knees included, to the foot pegs. Can you picture that? You can if you have a rich interior life. I also thought about using the chainsaw to write the lyrics to that old Elton John song *Sorry Seems To Be The Hardest Word* all over the old fart in hieroglyphics. Those are just two examples.

As close as I ever came to actually accosting King Putt was leaving the same note on his SUV as he made the rounds of his miniature golf courses. The note said, "I was here and you were gone. Now you are here and I am gone. Soon, I will be here but you will be gone-gone. Think about it." Mr. Amusement Park wasn't a very bright boy, but after a while I'd put the spook into him. All this took about two months.

During this period I was not only thinking of bringing a little karmic justice into King Putt's life. I was thinking about Rosiland Mammon too. I can't tell you how many times I picked up the phone to tell her I thought she was the most beautiful woman I'd ever seen and that what I felt for her was etcetera, etcetera, blah, blah, blah. But I just don't have the skills. I did see her though, five nights in a row, in the Little Theater musical version of *Othello*. She was wonderful. Every night I sat near the back and by the time the performance was over my turtleneck was wet with tears, tears of hate and sorrow. The hate surfaced when the main dude, a guy I sort of identified with some of the time, *strangled* my Rosiland, at which point all I could see was a guy with a Harley tattoo on his forearm. The tears of sorrow, well, who the hell knows where they came from. But somehow, after seeing the play five times, I couldn't quite picture myself carrying out my initial plan for King Putt, which I'm not going to describe to you since I didn't actually pull it off. I'll leave that to your rich interior life.

Still, I had to get even. He had to pay. I had to make the statement that my Rosiland couldn't make for herself, my Rosiland with the suffering look of a silent film star, my Rosiland who had endured five tragic Shakespearian deaths in as many nights.

If you've ever been to a King Putt miniature course, you can skip over this part because I'm just going to tell a little about them. First they have eighteen holes. Each is a par two. Each hole is basically a slab of concrete of different sizes and shapes covered with outdoor carpet and framed by a wooden two-by-four border to keep the ball on the course. Some holes have pyramids that you must putt the ball through. Others have a sphinx with a swinging tail you must avoid. One is a kneeling lion on a steep slope. The cat has a big open mouth that you putt the ball into, a belly that the ball rolls around in for a while before it comes out his butt, and if you're lucky, into the cup. There are mummies, and tombs, and pharaohs, fake palm trees—you get the idea.

Anyway, that's what I'm looking at in Rock Hill, South Carolina at three in the morning with my chainsaw in hand. I'm waiting for my rich interior mind to give me a sign. Because I'm thinking of myself now as a serial chainsaw specialist. My goal is to hit them all, but not all at once. My goal is to have an MO so Biker Brat knows these are not just fluke events. My crimes must escalate, you know, so they make a good story; and they have to be reasonable surprises so that as you go along you don't see it coming, but when you do see it you say to yourself, I should have seen that coming. All this explaining just exhausts me.

Attack number one. First the two-by-fours and only the two-by-fours. I cut them from around every hole and hauled them away.

I was there the next morning, standing with a church group of ten-year-olds, a busload from Charlotte, when the Rock Hill manager phoned the king of King Putts. The kids and I were waiting inside when the Harley rumbled up. After the two men entered the office to call the police, I passed around putters and balls.

"Damn, buddy," one of the Baptist youths said, "kinda hot to be wearing a turtleneck, ain't it?"

Outside, the balls flew off the tees, slamming into pyramids and pharaohs, ricocheting from concrete like a giant pinball machine.

I tapped on the glass to the office and the two men turned from the phone. "What's par for this course?" I said. But before they could answer two crying kids rushed up, one with his front teeth in his open palm, the other with a purple knot between his eyes that made him look like a baby unicorn.

I slipped my lawyer's business card into their pockets as I was leaving.

A few weeks later at the Columbia King Putt, I began by chainsawing away the two-by-fours, but this time I added the head of the lion with the big mouth to my take. In Spartanburg, I left with the two-by-fours, the lion's head, and the five pharaohs. Add to the aforementioned mummies from the Myrtle Beach King Putt. After each attack I was there to pass around putters and my lawyer's business card.

I began reading about the work of Vapor in *The State* newspaper, and by the time I'd left my mark at the Myrtle Beach King Putt, the local media had picked up the story. One morning while having my coffee, as I have for ten years, at the Venus Pancake House where nobody knows me, I opened the paper to see that a musical version of a play called *A Doll's House* was coming to the Little Theater and that none other than Rosiland Mammon had been cast in the leading role. I was there of course for every show, again in the back row. But this time, at the end of the performance when Rosiland tap dances to the door singing a little number called "Adios, Mother Fucker" to Helmer, the Harley guy in this one, I stood and pumped my fist and shouted, Whoo! Whoo! Whoo! Whoo! until the usher told me to hold it down.

I knew that the Charleston King Putt would be a challenge. I had lost what you might call the element of surprise. But when I walked out of the theater that Saturday night, I knew I had to do it.

Call me a believer in end-of-the world scenarios if you want, but I watched the weather and I prayed and whispered, "Ros-i-land-Mam-mon, Ros-i-land-Mam-mon, like Sugar-plum-fairy," over and over.

And my wish came true. I rented a U-Haul and drove to Charleston and waited for the hurricane to take out the electricity. Then I cranked my chainsaw and went to work. This time I came back to Darlington with even the signature King Putt fake palms.

Out near Irby Street in front of Red Meat Rally, I recognized the fancy trailer with the Harley decal and the For Sale sign. Victory was mine, but for what? My sense of satisfaction soon passed. I was left with a garage full of King Putt and a heart full of love for Rosiland Mammond. And no way of making use of any of it.

At work, mid-February is crunch time. I'm so busy arranging flowers that the week kind of becomes one long day. I even get my Venus Pancake coffee to go, not that anybody there knows the difference. So I'm up to my elbows in boutonnieres and bouquets when I hear a customer say he's come to pick up flowers for the closing performance at the Little Theater. Because my rich interior life takes a backseat to work around Valentine's Day, the news doesn't immediately sink in. But then it hits me, and I find the newspaper. Sure enough it's my Rosiland Mammon starring in the final night's performance of the musical, *Helen Keller*.

When I arrive at the theater, the performance is sold out. I show the woman at the ticket counter a fresh hundred, but she just points to the Fire Marshall's maximum occupancy sign and shakes her head. Outside alone I listen to the singing. I recognize Rosiland's voice and imagine in my rich interior mind her lovely feet tapping and spinning and the astonished eyes of the audience as Helen Keller leaps and lands.

Then a kind of darkness fills me.

I can't stay there. So I sit in my truck for a while with my rich blah, blah, blah. Then I close my eyes and fight that black-vat-rising feeling before the bad pictures begin. I head them off with my heart's picture of Rosiland Mammon, and then I have an idea and fire up the truck.

Time is running out but I work like a Turk. I know that's not very original. Besides what do I know about a Turk? But if you're still with me you're probably used to my conversational failures. Let's say I work like a Canadian. With the help of a powerful will and a rich interior mind, I get the job done then drive back to the Little Theater.

My heart drops as I pull into the dark lot and see that it's almost empty. In my days as Vapor, I'd been to lots of cast parties, which always went on for hours. But this, I suddenly realize, is Valentine's night.

I parked near the entrance. The doors opened and a man I recognized as the play's director and his wife held hands and weaved toward their car. I drew a deep breath and the fragrance of four dozen roses filled my lungs. The effect is not the same if you work as a florist. I looked down at my callused and blistered hands. Then I stepped from my truck carrying the four dozen roses across my outstretched arms like an offering and started toward the theater door. One thing you ought to know about those of us who believe in end-of-the-world scenarios: we can believe in just about anything. And so it is that as I approach the locked door, I'm certain that Rosiland is on the other side of it on her way to meet me.

And so it was. When she opened the door, I stood in the dim street light bearing roses. She walked straight for me, arms extended like Helen Keller. I knelt before her. But instead of taking the flowers, she lifted her hands and touched my face. I feel their soft warmth bathe my closed eyes, my lips, and I hear her breathy voice of wonder, and when I open my eyes I see that Rosiland's are closed. There is a single luminous tear on her cheek.

I don't know how long we'd have remained like that, just the two of us, draped in the scent of roses on that balmy South Carolina night in February, had it not been for the blue lights and the sirens.

I'll admit that I was a little shaky when the cop put the cuffs on me, but I had enough sense to request that John Truett, my lawyer, be present before answering any questions, and by the time I stood in the blinding lights of the line-up, I was a new and happy man. You couldn't wipe the bliss from my face, given the picture in my rich interior mind, the picture of Rosiland's smile and her happy tears when she arrived home to discover the palm trees and the fairways filled with rose petals. I was thinking of nothing else.

And pulling off the turtleneck before they brought us out for identification hadn't been, as my lawyer said, a brilliant move. I was just sweating in that tiny interrogation room and thinking of nothing but Rosiland Mammon.

It was later, at the Venus Pancake House, after John described the witnesses' reactions to the scars, after I was free and clear, only then, when I'd stopped thinking for a minute about Rosiland Mammon, when I was no longer feeling her touch, that I began to put the pieces together, all I had seen and felt, the guilt and sorrow, the joy and laughter, only then that it all began to make sense.

Pete

It *is* the way patients on the operating table describe it. "I floated up. Way up there," they say. "Below I saw the surgeon's bloody hands lift my severed heart and drop it into the beer cooler." Way up there, that's where I was, teetering on my knees, looking down at myself and at Russ Watts as he smeared his tears and considered knocking me back to La-La Land.

"Where is she, Pete?" he said raising his fist. From up in the stars, I saw myself below, kneeling in the wedge of Russ' headlights. Our identical pickups—green with shiny steel vault like toolboxes against their cabs—were parked in a dark empty field. Farther back, near I-95, hung the lighted billboard for my plumbing company: Pete Hump's Heat Pumps, it said.

Chloe's breath teased my ear. Had I not spilled so much blood I'd be getting some rising action down in my whanger. But instead, I was suddenly flushed down to the ground again, there on my knees, ticktocking this way and that, bound hand and foot, staring into the blinding headlights of Russ' truck. Russ, my ex-best friend, the guy I'd hired to do industrial work, walked circles around me, gesturing up to the heavens, mumbling to the Almighty. He stopped and slowly craned down face to face. His breath smelled like hotdog chili and bourbon.

"Let's skip the question this time, Pete."

I came to a swaying stop. Turning to my right, I saw Chloe sitting beside me on a porch swing. She smiled and ran her hand up my thigh. "Pete Hump's heat pumps," she purred. I was in love with her, this woman whose idea of housework was opening the mail, this woman with a mouth you'd take a beating for too. Chloe. Chloe, Russ' wife.

Russ' fist struck my jaw with the force of jackhammer. I wobbled like a giant top and watched as his ghostly figure entered the headlights then disappeared. From way off I heard the pickup's engine turn over. Russ hit the high beams, and in that blinding, electrifying instant I thought of Chloe's thigh against my cheek, smooth as warm milk. The headlights began to fidget. He's decided to put a bumper through my brain.

I should have known something was up at The Paradise Lounge, where we drink. Russ chased the last bite of his hotdog with half a bourbon then turned his blank eyes down into the paper hotdog tray.

"Why won't she cook?" he said to himself.

"Beats me," I said to myself.

I guess it was something in the tone of my voice.

Russ oozed from his barstool and zombied over to the jukebox. I didn't think about it at the time.

Everybody at the bar turned. The Righteous Brothers' *You've Lost That Loving Feeling* blasted from the speakers. Russ rocked like a lunatic and sang loud and unrighteously. He lifted his glass, signaling George Miles for his fifth drink. After three minutes, The Brothers faded, but not Russ. He kept shouting that the feelin' was gone, gone, gone. His eyes went all bubbly. He threw back his drink, then zigzagged across the dance floor and dropped onto the barstool beside me. He reached for the fresh bourbon.

In the mirror behind the bar, I watched as he bowed his head. His eyes studied the bottom of his glass. It went down forever. As he lifted the drink to his lips, Russ froze, as if a message from the spirits suddenly arrived special delivery. Slowly, like a mechanical toy winding down, he set the glass on the bar. His eyes shot up into the mirror, ricocheted into mine.

"Beats me," he whispered, turning towards me in that machinelike way, his red eyes like underwater flares.

Russ lifted his foot from the accelerator and silence rushed in. Then inside the cab, Brother Bill Medley sang about the loss of that loving feeling. Behind the wheel, Russ' black silhouette wailed that he could not go on, on, on.

The shifting of the transmission sounded like the dry firing of a revolver. His blinding headlights inched forward before creeping to a predatory halt. The smell of grease was in the air, and the heat from the engine worked the edges of my bleeding face like a metal file.

I heard the sound of the steel lid of the vault toolbox open and swallowed hard as I considered its contents: the claw hammers, one with a wooden handle, the other one rubber coated; the one-pound sledge, as blunt-faced and deadly as a rabid pit bull; and the masonry hammer, sleek and sexy. His choice would determine the number and size of my skull bits.

Beside me, Russ stood at attention facing the spray of headlights.

I glanced at his fist. No hammer. Looking down on me, he slowly opened the fingers of his right hand, serving up a roll of soldering wire in his palm. I'd seen enough Martin Scorsese movies to know what a length of wire can do to a man's throat. I heaved a breath that drew a bead of blood back up into my nose. A cold numbness ran up my thighs. My testicles scurried backwards like hermit crabs.

"If you don't tell me where to find her, I'm gonna kill you Pete." He was still crying. I could hear it in his voice. "I love her, Pete," he said in a sniffling voice.

"Me too," I said.

He loomed above me panting and growling, amping his anger, then turned and lifted the hood of the truck. Resting the coil of wire on the radiator, Russ hovered over the engine as if he were studying its design. He reached for the wire. After a few seconds, he began slowly backing toward me like a man with a dynamite lead, letting out the wire he'd attached to the throttle arm. He bore down on me, paused, then pulled the wire. The engine revved until the headlights quivered.

Murder/suicide, I thought. Pete Hump's Plumbing Truck Kills Owner and Partner, the headlines would read. I fought the duct tape binding my ankles and wrists. My hands were mittens. I couldn't feel my toes.

Then I smelled the rotten scent of panic.

I was going to die. My brains would be hammered out, either before or after I was strangled with soldering wire, and I would be squashed, either with or without my partner, by a truck I was still making payments on. Either way, I wouldn't make a very handsome corpse for Chloe, the woman who refused to cook for me, the woman who broke eggs into a mixing dish, dropped her vibrator into the bowl, then picked up her towel and suntan lotion and walked out of the kitchen, saying "I hope you like'em scrambled." Chloe, who pressed her nails into my chest, tossed back her wild, blonde hair, shut her eyes and rode me like a Harley and twenty miles of bad road.

For Chloe, I would die. Yes, I thought, for Chloe I would die.

Then I saw the jumper cables.

Their heavy copper jaws slowly opened and closed in Russ' fists. He held them at arm's length like two angry cobras then brought their heads together. Sparks sent splotches of eerie yellow light up into Russ' savage face.

"It's throw-down time," he whispered. "I'm gonna splatter your fuckin' brains all over the ground. Then, when they stop smoking, I'm gonna sort through the goop until I find the answers I'm looking for."

He wasn't crying anymore.

Against the stark headlights, he lumbered toward me, a viper in each hand, his towering figure growing like a giant shadow. He brought the cable heads together in slow gruesome applause. Stuttering, ticking bright flashes of electric venom blazed from his fists. I closed my eyes, bowed my head. Russ stood beside me like a sentry, the only sounds his breathing and the murmur of the truck's engine. He shifted both cables into his left hand. The colliding metal heads hissed and sparked. His free hand lifted the solder wire connected to the throttle arm.

"Pete," he said, "in my professional opinion, we need more juice. I really want this to be an electrifying moment, I really do." He tugged the wire. The sound of the engine ascended an octave. The viper head clamps erupted with fire. Even with eyes shut tight, I saw the blinding flashes. Russ tapped the flaming ends of the cables on top of my head. I heard the crackle and smelled the burn.

"I know you're in there, Chloe," he said in a singsong voice. "Come out come out, wherever you are."

There's a noise a dog makes when he needs to eat grass, a sort of rotor rooter surging in his throat. I was making that sound.

"I'd-tell-ya-if-I-knew-I'd-tell-ya-I-would-if-I-knew—."

Russ leaned down face to face, dangling the jumper cables over my head.

"Yoooo-hoooo?" he said in a voice from some other world. Revving the engine, he brought one of the copperhead clamps in front of my eyes, squeezing its jaws open then letting it slowly shut. The mouth gaped, and my eyes followed as the open jaws curved out of sight.

Its dagger-like teeth entered the flesh of my right ear.

Russ pulled the wire tighter. The truck shook like a bad case of DTs.

"I'd-tell-ya-if-I-knew-I-would—"

"You know, Pete, a heavy dose of current might reroute your circuits just enough for you to remember where she is."

"I'd-tell-ya-if-I-knew—"

"You wanna know what happens when I clamp this other ear? Go ahead, make an educated guess." He pulled on the wire like a trolling line. The engine whined, Wa-WOWWW-Wa! Wa-WOWWW-Wa! He had to yell over the noise. "Think it kinda-like pro-jectiles your jelly brain out the top of your fuckin' head?"

The electrical force field surrounding the open copper jaws tingled the tiny hairs of my left ear. I could sense the slow contraction of the razor-sharp teeth.

"Hawthorne Apartments," I blurted, "West Side of Charleston, near where the interstates cross, apartment 212, the one with the red door. You'll see the Mustang out front."

"That wasn't the question I asked you, Pete. What I asked was if you wanted to know what happens when I jump start your shit-for-brains; that was the question I asked."

I was making that loud dog-gotta-eat-some-grass sound again.

"I take that as a no, Pete. *This* is what happens."

Russ pulled back hard on the wire lead. The force of the truck's engine made the earth tremble beneath me. I couldn't hear my screams over its roaring whine. The instant the second clamp closed down onto my left ear, my eyes shot open. Blood trickled down onto my neck. Maybe, I thought, there is a buildup in there before the current erupts like a flamethrower from the top of my head.

A couple of seconds passed. No electricity, no explosion.

Then Russ and I were eyeball to eyeball. The hotdog chili and bourbon had formed an epoxy relationship on his breath.

"It's a good thing you chose plumbing not electrical, Pete. A damned good thing. You stupid fuck. You don't know your AC from your DC."

Russ squeezed open the clamps and took a step back. He held the cables' heads together. Flashes of fire made a hog's snout of his nostrils and dug out the hollows of his eyes, forming empty black craters. Laughing like a nutcase, he disconnected the cables from the battery terminals of Pete Hump's Plumbing truck #2.

Russ walked from the darkness back toward me, taking shape as he entered the headlights again.

And for the last time I saw his right hand form a fist.

From blackness I descended to a soft landing. I lay on my back. One of my eyes opened a little more than the other. Above, the stars had all disappeared. I'm not sure what time it was, but the grass was shiny and cool with dew. Feeling had returned to my fingers and toes. While I'd been away, my unbound legs and arms had resumed their natural positions. The blood around my nose had dried, but when I peeled it away I felt a warm, fresh drip. Slowly, tentatively, I stood, feeling that if I didn't balance my body just so, my head might fall off my shoulders.

For spite I guess, Russ had left the jumper cables and *The Righteous Brothers Greatest Hits* on the passenger seat of Pete Hump's # 1.

With the kind of clarity and intensity I've heard combat soldiers describe, I drove the ten miles to the hunting cabin. From Pocket Road I turned onto the pine straw covered path that wormed its way nearly a mile through a canopy of deep woods. The straw silenced the tires and the thick brush absorbed the sound of the engine.

I left the truck running and its lights on.

The cabin faced Black Creek. I'd helped Russ dig a well and put in an old-fashioned hand pump. There I'd first seen Chloe, sunbathing on the narrow sandbar that jutted out into the dark water.

Inside the cabin, I reached above the sink for the large coffee can where Russ hid the Smith & Wesson 357. In a tiny closet, I found his hunting jacket and my deer knife in one pocket. The shovel would be outside under the porch.

I lifted the Brother's *Greatest Hits* CD from the passenger seat, tucked it in the coat pocket with the knife and tossed the jacket over the cables.

When I turned back onto Pocket Road, it was 2:30, the moon the crimson color of my left eye. I wasn't sure if Russ was still in Charleston, but he'd had time to get there and break into our love nest. At the pay phone outside the IGA grocery, I dialed the number for the Charleston Police Department and reported what sounded to me like a burglary at the Hawthorne Apartments, number 212. If Russ was there, bloody knuckles and all, he'd have a long story to tell the cops. If not, he would be getting back into town before dawn. Either way, he'd be back. The best I could hope for was later rather than sooner.

In high school, Russ and I had gone to the state football championship together. We won the game on a play Coach called "the bait-and-switch," a misdirection play. We were like brothers. Now we were the mightiest of foes, playing for the highest of stakes, the love of a beautiful woman. The bait had to be good, the switch brilliant. Time on the game clock was winding down.

The service road along I-95 splintered off into smaller paths used to maintain the giant billboard. Thanks to its bright lights, I wouldn't be seen in its shadow. I parked, shut off the engine and felt for the .357 and the bowie knife. I glanced at what was left of my face in the mirror.

I jammed the Greatest Hits CD against the rear tire. Bait.

26

The new steel toolbox that stretched the width of my truck bed was unlocked. I lifted the lid.

"Get out," I said.

A stark look of horror remained frozen upon Chloe's face as she slowly levitated from the steel vault. I reached for the pistol and backed away. Chloe didn't speak. Night was shutting down, and the engine's cooling contracting metal sounded like the muffled breaking of bones. I motioned for her to step down from the truck. Her eyes narrowed as she studied the cuts and bruises, thinking I suppose, that Russ had maybe knocked my nose upside down. "Go on now," I said, signaling for her to move to the front of the truck.

She stood facing me. "Take your clothes off," I said.

She resisted. But not for long.

The digging was fast and easy.

Her panties were still damp and warm. I wiped down the knife and pistol with them, then tossed the blade into the brush nearby. I would deposit the clean .357 in the ditch beside the service road before I pulled onto the interstate. After running my fingers over her panties one last time, I dropped them in the shallow trough and reached again for the shovel.

Bait.

When I was done, I slid the shovel up the truck bed, dropped the cables and my gloves into the toolbox then sat on the tailgate to catch my breath. I looked up at the enormous billboard over my head. Pete Hump's Heat Pumps, it said. I thought about Russ and my future-former-best-friend's wife. Misdirection, I thought. You think all is well. Then, wham, out of nowhere, blindsided. Blitzed. Never saw it coming.

Switch.

When I opened the truck door, the interior light softly glowed around my sleeping Chloe, who lay nestled in the corner, knees folded up inside the hunting jacket. The coat didn't quite cover one shoulder, and the light flowed down from her tangled blonde hair, over her jaw, to her tanned shoulder.

I started the engine and shifted into drive, heard the crunch of The Brothers' CD, the shattering of that lovin' feeling. She woke.

"The bra and panties were a Valentine's present," she said, pulling back her hair, exposing the crescent of one breast. "Remember?"

I didn't.

I said, "The cops will need to find something with your bodily fluids on it, like maybe a big knife that belongs to Russ. The police dogs will find the bra and panties. He'll have a lot of explaining to do. A jealous husband can be a dangerous thing, you know."

Chloe studied the remains of my face. "Looks like it," she said.

She turned, resting her shoulders against the window, knees up, pressing her toes into my thigh. Before I veered off the service road, I tossed Russ' printless pistol into the shallow ditch for easy detection, then took the cloverleaf.

"How far do you think we'll get?" she said.

"Pretty far," I said.

"I wore the panties special," she said.

"I'll get you another pair."

"For Valentine's?"

"Sure."

"And candlelight? Soft music?"

"Maybe," I said.

"A new life? Promise?"

I glanced in the mirror.

"What about you?" she said. "What would you like?" Her toes dug into me. Her knees slowly opened and closed like a butterfly's wings. The jacket lay open.

"For Valentines, you mean?"

She smiled up at me again. "Say candlelight, soft music, a hot bath and wine."

"A home cooked meal." I hit the blinker and stepped on the gas. "A back rub and a cold beer."

"Oh," she said, drawing her knees up to her chest, looking out at the passing night. Glancing down at the speedometer, I let up on the gas a little. I didn't want to get blindsided by blue lights.

"Which way are we going?" she said.

"West."

"Don't feel like it," she said, speaking out into the night.

I thought of the bait and switch.

Turning away, she tilted her cheek against the glass and closed her eyes. The truck cab was quiet.

We were racing ahead on the interstate now, leaving what I thought was the world behind. We had a direction but no destination. A now but not a then. And I'd only begun to feel the weight of the miles in front of us when I saw the signs of her first tears.

28

Nick and Dave

While waiting at the bar for two women they didn't know, Nick Granger and his brother Dave exchanged *but* stories.

"Here's one for you," Nick said. He tilted his beer then set down the mug. "*She* said, 'It was terribly wrong of me not to tell you I'm married, *but—*.'"

His brother Dave wasn't impressed. "*This*," he said, "is my former wife: 'It's not that I don't love you, I swear, David, *but—*.'"

Nick signaled to the bartender, B.B. "Let's call that our segue to sex humor, brother," he said. "Try this one on for size. My doctor talking." Nick lowered his voice an octave. "We will, of course, have to wait for the lab results, *but—*."

"Oooooh," Dave said. The brothers laughed.

Behind them, the happy hour crowd was filing in, each patron with his or her own *but* story to tell: I would have made that sale today, but—. Or, I know that he's not the man for me, but—. Or, I promised myself I'd never set foot in here again, but—.

The Paradise Lounge was part sanctuary part asylum where irreconcilables held hands and bellied up to the bar. Where regulars and first-timers alike reconstructed office politics and exorcised credit card debt, where marriage counseling slowly began to make sense, or not. Where the bar was as close to an altar as some would likely get. A temporary holding zone where their lives weren't a mix-and-match thrift store of contradictions. Where Dale Earnhardt never died. Where they'd come from where they hide, their rendezvous with the irrational. A refuge, where barstool neighbors exchanged covenants of devotion and lies, rolled up their sleeves and chiseled away at the granite cliff of history, their only tool that single conjunction, *but*.

The two women, a real estate agent Nick had met and the woman's friend, a cosmetics rep, were late. Nick, who had set up the blind date for his brother, looked at his watch. "They said they'd be here at six."

"*However*," Dave said, lifting his beer, smiling. Dave was rebounding from divorce.

Nick dialed a number. "We'll be there for you," sang a real estate jingle before the machine picked up. It was six-thirty. Nick left a message. "We could have gotten our times crossed up," he said. Nick was an algebra teacher. His older brother sold software.

"Maybe we got our *lives* mixed up," Dave said into the bottom of his beer mug. He'd married a girl he'd gotten pregnant in college, setting into motion a series of unhappy calamities, each a product of Dave's doing the right thing. His had become a *but* life. Now his confidence was a little low. "Our times mixed up? I don't even know what *day* it is," Dave said.

Nick lifted his glass, signaled for another round and smiled at B.B., the finely crafted red-haired bartender. He and Dave adored her from afar in high school. Over the years, both men privately lusted for her. But she was, after all, Coach's wife. "What day *is* it?" Dave said.

Nick looked away. A reflective pause crossed his face.

"What?" Dave said. "*What?*"

"Today is the anniversary of Dad's death," Nick said. The lovely bartender set the beers before them. "Thanks, B.B.," Nick said.

"Here's to you, Pop," Dave said, raising his glass. "Speaking of mixed up, that guy took the trophy." They both drank.

"Funny," Nick said, "That reminds me. I dreamed about him the other night. I'd forgotten this. I was near Asheville looking for a place to live, and I saw him in a '38 convertible coupe, top down. His hair was in this really goofy do, curled tight and piled up like a big metal spring on top of his head, dyed black except the ends which were blond. He gave me a look that said he'd done it as a gag."

"A laugh a minute, huh? A real clown, that one."

"He was headed out of town. I knew in the dream he was dying, you know. I mean, I knew what the dream meant as I was dreaming it. I wanted to go with him."

"That sounds like you, all right," Dave said. Nick looked up from his drink to his brother. Dave looked away. "Don't worry bro, you'll get there."

Nick said, "He was headed west. I told him to step on it. I said maybe he could out-drive the sun."

Dave wouldn't look at him.

Then Dave said to his beer, "My guess is we played maybe forty, fifty football games in high school, right?"

"Including playoffs, something like that. Why?" Nick said.

"Daddy-O never showed up for a single one. Not one."

Standing at the urinal in the men's room, Nick felt the building quake then heard the shouting and confusion that followed. Back in the bar, he saw the backs of the swarming crowd. Vincent Howle, who was celebrating another release from the county jail, shouted above the cries, "It's a sign from God! It's a sign from God!" Nick saw his brother. Dave stood on his bar stool looking beyond the clustered heads, nodding in disbelief at the front end of a '66 Mustang that had crashed through the large plate glass window of The Paradise Lounge.

"What happened?" Nick shouted over the noise. Dave turned to B.B., who was all elbows near the front, tunneling through the crowd. Nick was beside Dave now. The Mustang's fish eye headlights were raised to the heavens. One of its front wheels was slowly turning like a dying clock.

"How'd he *do* that?" Nick said.

"Good thing it was a Mustang," Dave said looking down at his brother. "That long hood, that's where the glass fell."

B.B. screamed a curse above the noise, and in a matter of seconds silence blanketed the room. "Coach," somebody whispered. Nick and Dave wedged their way to the door.

"Huddle-up, men," a slurred voice repeated. "Huddle-up."

Outside, B.B. stood hands on hips. Excited patrons poured from the bar, surrounding the car, which looked like the down side of a seesaw. A guy in a turtleneck helped Coach out of the car. Coach leaned back, steadying himself. He studied his wife's face as he lit a cigarette. He lifted his arm and spoke to the crowd. "As God is my witness," he said, "I love this woman more than life itself." B.B. lifted her hands, covered her eyes. Sirens echoed from the west. She couldn't look at him. He spotted Dave and Nick. "What'll it be boys?" he said. "I say we go with the single wing. When all is lost, it's all that's left."

The sirens were closer. B.B. swiped her tears. They saw the pleading in her eyes.

"Come on," Nick said to his brother.

Coach sat in the center of the backseat, looking out like an inquisitive tourist. On Highway 52 toward Society Hill, they passed manicured fields of cotton, corn and soybeans. By the full moon's light you could see everything, the long, clean rows, the black earth, the tree line that billowed like dark clouds on the horizon.

Nick and Dave had been the backfield that championship year, B.B. head cheerleader. The brothers were ushers at Coach and B.B.'s wedding the following summer. And for a long, long time Coach and B.B. had been everybody's happiness, the kind of happiness you await and expect, the kind you want for yourself and for others. The kind you believe will last forever.

But now Darlingtonians hung their heads and spoke in whispers. About Coach and the smart-ass hoodlum who had urinated on the championship banner, cursed and spat upon Coach. The trial that followed. The verdict. Coach's drinking. And about the horror in The Paradise Lounge the night two men from Charlotte burned The Main Street Convenience Store. About B.B. and another man. Some still shielded their hearts with the thin armor of denial, saying to themselves and to each other that B.B. and Coach's love would prevail, that rumors are never far from a woman with B.B.'s looks, especially if she works in a bar. Especially when her husband drinks.

"Where to, Coach?" Dave said, looking back in his mirror. Coach leaned forward and passed a twenty to Nick.

"Let's ride as long as we can, boys. It'll be a while before I see much of the outdoors, I suspect."

At the interstate, Dave pulled into the SAV-WAY. Nick went inside for a 12-pack. Coach craned this way and that, taking it all in like a happy vacationer.

"Look," Dave said, pointing toward a billboard a half mile down the interstate. The sign said, Pete Hump's Heat Pumps. Pete, an HVAC guy now, had played linebacker on that championship team.

"He's a drunk," Coach said.

Nick tore open the 12-pack and passed a beer, along with the twenty, back to Coach.

"Keep it," Coach said.

"No," Dave said.

"Do what I say," said Coach. But Nick laid the money on the backseat.

"Where to?" Dave said. They both turned to Coach.

"Suit yourself," he said.

Nick handed his brother a beer.

The floorboards softly clanged with empties as Dave eased into a sharp curve, destination Dovesville, the home of Flat Nose the famous tree-climbing dog. It was Coach's idea to pay a visit to the K-9 celebrity of The Johnny Carson Show. But Dave spotted a state trooper parked in the shadow of the old Hanes' plant. He took a right at Spring. Nobody was saying anything. Up ahead at the end of double skid marks stood what was left of the sign for Pharaoh.

"Take me to my pyramid," Coach said, smiling now.

"Yes, Your Highness," Dave said.

"That would be Your Lowness, to you, son," Coach said.

"Yes, sir," said Dave.

The three men ascended the steps of the steep cement bleachers. Nick carried the beer. Dave steadied Coach. At the very top of the stadium, Coach sat between his former players studying the empty field, drinking his beer. Overhead the sky was etched with long grey skids of clouds, a decoy for rain that wouldn't come.

"The thing about the single wing is that it gives power to the little guy," Coach said. "When you're out-manned, that's what you've got to go with. I call it the offense of the Confederacy. It makes a shell game of it for the defense. You throw everything at a soft spot in the line. Worked at Chickamauga." He drank. His eyes panned the deserted playing field. "Single wing," he whispered. "By then the war was lost."

They were silent. Radiant moonlight cast shadows like hooded monks upon the white cement bleachers. Below lay the glittering wet gridiron, the hundred-yard stretch where they had once bled and cursed, tasted victory and ascended to nobility. Where they had felt loved. "All it takes is a blocking back who don't mind getting his nose bloody," Coach said. He threw his right arm over Nick's shoulder. "And a tailback with a fake lateral and a half-decent arm." He reached for Dave.

"And a Coach," Nick said.

"Formula for a state championship," Dave said.

"Nah," Coach said, slowly bending his eyes from goal line to goal line. "For that you need a woman you love, a woman who loves you."

They were traveling again.

"It's first and ten in the red zone," Coach said, "and we're out of beer, boys." Nick and Dave exchanged a quick look. "There's still time on the clock," Coach said, smiling. "Let's go for it."

"Coach—" Dave said. His boss had scheduled a morning meeting to discuss continuous improvement and his lagging productivity projections.

"Have to pee," Coach said.

Dave and Nick sat outside the SAV-WAY silently considering their options. Nick's math students would smell the alcohol on his breath. There was no getting around that. He only hoped Riley, the principal, would be too busy to call him in before lunch.

They looked up. Coach wavered in the bright lights as he paid for another 12-pack. Outside, he lumbered toward the car, horizon-to-horizon grin on his face, twenty pounds heavier, but with that gait they'd followed up and down the sidelines when everything rested on his next decision. He climbed in and leaned forward over the seat between Nick and Dave, then rested a gentle hand on the shoulder of each. "You're my boys," he said. "Always have been."

"Where to?" Dave said. Nick opened another beer for his brother.

Dave knew driving near town was risky on account of how drunk he was, but he also knew that on account of how drunk he was he'd better not drift too far from home. *But*, he thought. "I have to sober up a little," Dave said. They were on the old Mechanicsville Highway. "Get some air."

"Take Cashua Ferry," Nick said.

Dave pulled onto Country Club Drive then parked in the empty lot beneath the slanted shadow of the clubhouse, near the tennis courts. Coach slept in back.

"I need to walk," Dave said.

Together the brothers laid out Coach in the backseat in case the cops showed. By now they'd know that Nick and Dave had taken him from the scene of the accident. By now the cops knew everything.

The brothers walked the first fairway.

"Remember the last time we were here?" Nick said.

"No," Dave said.

"A couple of days before Dad died."

"His last ride," Dave said.

"Getting him into the car that day?" Nick said.

"He spilled water all over himself, didn't he?" Dave said. "Given his capacity for cursing, I thought the guy had the strength to live forever."

They turned when they saw headlights over the bunker, watched the lights come to a stop. They waited a few seconds then started back.

"He wanted to drive out and tell his golf buddies goodbye," Nick said. "He wanted to tell them he was dying, but—. What happened? Where was everybody?"

"That was the day the pro's son killed himself," Dave said. "Remember? Dad thought there was going to be a tournament, that he'd get the final spotlight, his last chance at being a wheelchair big shot, but—."

"That's not what he thought. The man was dying for Christ's sake," Nick said. He stopped and looked at his brother.

Dave turned his back to the moonlight, his face suddenly shrouded in darkness. "Considering how he always treated you—."

Nick grabbed his brother's shirt, both fists knotted up in front. "*Damn* you," he whispered, "Damn you."

"Damn him," Dave said. "What he did to Mom?"

"Or what she didn't do for him? Sometimes it's what you should do but don't, brother."

"Like now, brother?" Dave said. In his tight fists Nick felt the anger rising in Dave's chest.

Intertwined, they stood in the bunker's shadow. A long moment. Then, "You must be drunk," Nick whispered, dropping his hands. He walked away.

After crossing the eighteenth green, they stopped and looked over at the car as if expecting an ambush. But all was quiet and peaceful. "I'll drive," Nick said. "I'd like to drive, you know, in case—."

"How's your insurance?" Dave asked. He knew the answer.

"I'm okay," Nick said.

He started the car. Coach lay curled in the backseat. "We never could have imagined it would come to this, could we?" Dave said. The question hung in the air. He drew a deep breath, blew it out. He lifted the beer box. There were two beers inside. They looked back at sleeping Coach and opened the beers.

"Where to?" Nick said.

The moon was lower, brighter, and Nick took the turns without headlights, driving at a creep. Coach snored.

The headstones, like soft, luminous blinking eyes, flickered pale blue in the moonlight.

"Do you know where you are?" Dave said.

Nick didn't answer. Then, "I'm sorry, but you'll have to help me."

They softly pushed their car doors shut. Nick led. Dave followed. Then they stood shoulder to shoulder at the marker.

"You should have been there when he died," Nick said. Dave was looking at his father's name etched in granite. "He didn't take fluids for two days, nothing," Nick said. "You should have seen how blue his eyes were. We sprayed the inside of his mouth, it was so dry. But when he took his last breath, there was this huge tear that formed. One tear. They say the soul lives in the eyes. You should have been there to see how blue they were. You should have." Dave looked at him. "No excuse," Nick said. He started back for the car, leaving his brother standing over the grave.

Nearing the car they saw the silhouette of Coach in the backseat sitting straight and tall.

"You all right?" Dave asked, bending forward at his window.

Coach didn't answer, just sat up soldier tall, a wide grin across his face. "Hand me the keys, Nick," Dave said.

"I'll drive," Nick said. "You know what's going down, right?"

"For the count." Coach mumbled.

Dave held out his hand.

"No," Nick said.

Dave reached for his brother's keys. "Please," he said.

Dave parked on Hampton Street, a couple of blocks from The Paradise Lounge. "Here's the key to my car," he said. "Don't be in a hurry to bail us out." He looked back at Coach. "Besides, I think I could sleep for a week." Nick took Dave's key.

He offered his hand. Dave took it.

Dave Granger pulled away from the curb slowly, cautiously, his full attention on the center line, reminding himself that he might be drunker than he felt, resolute that he would avoid blue lights, certain in his heart of hearts that he would get Coach home safely, that he had what it took to outrun the rising sun if necessary, that he would do this one thing for Coach. He would get him home, to his wife, who was surely there waiting for him.

Tami and Billie Jean

It was the Southern 500 race weekend and the checkout line at the Darlington IGA wasn't moving fast enough to suit Tami. She and Billie Jean had spent the afternoon lying out at Tami's trailer and the dog day sun had cooked them medium rare, perfect for a cold beer.

"They'll be hot by the time we get'em paid for," Tami announced, hoisting the 12-pack and giving Billie Jean a nod to say her comment was intended for the two young women ahead of them. The high schooler with the name Monique on the back of her purple T-shirt said to the cashier, "That boy ain't nothin'. Ever thing he's got, he's drivin' or wearin'? He ain't like he seem. He got issues."

Tami rolled her eyes heavenward. "I ain't what I seem, Lord," Tami murmured. "I got issues."

"But he pretty," the girl in front of her, O'blique, said. They wore the same purple T-shirt. The chunky pale blonde cashier with the dark brown roots and shiny braces who should have been ringing up Tami's purchase bobbleheaded in agreement. "But he's so material-lipstick," she said. "Ever thing he got, he's showin." The three bobbled in unison.

When the magic eye parted the IGA's doors for Tami and Billie Jean, a rush of hot air blew back their hair.

"It ain't the heat, it's the stupidity," Tami, the cropped blonde, said, staring straight ahead as she marched toward her truck. The two women wore identical faded Dale Earnhardt T-shirts over their bathing suits.

"You got room to talk about somebody messin' up the language," Billie Jean said, smiling. Billie Jean was taller and darker than Tami. She held her smile while Tami slid the key into the ignition, tore off the end of the beer box, tucked a cold one between her legs. "What?" Tami said to that smile. "*Whaaat?*" She passed a cold one over to Billie Jean, who wouldn't wipe away that smile.

"You got room to talk," Billie Jean said again.

"That don't count," Tami said. "Two letters don't count."

"The *hell* it don't," Billie Jean said, watching as a tight-lipped grin softened Tami's face. Tami and Billie Jean toasted their beers.

The night before on their way home from the Little Nashville Club, Tami suddenly pulled over at the Baptist Temple. It was two-thirty in the morning, the first night they'd been out drinking together. Tami shut off the engine. "A woman's gotsta do what a woman's gotsta do," she said. When she stepped from her truck, the church sign read President Bush We Pray For Your Election. But in the rearview mirror as they drove off, the sign read President Bush We Play For Your Erection.

Tami lit a cigarette, shifted into first gear and eased across the parking lot.

"But nobody likes it when you make fun of the way they talk," Billie Jean said, scanning the horizon for cops before she raised her beer. "It ain't right. Everybody's got a right to be who they are. Everybody's entitled. You won't like it tonight when some dude from New York tries to bait you into saying *y'all* for him, like some trick monkey."

"Depend on how pretty he is."

"You won't like it."

"You don't know much," Tami said with a smile. She looked at the front of Billie Jean's Earnhardt T-shirt. "And ever thing you got, you showing." Tami patted her thigh. "But you so *sweet*. You pretty, too."

By the time they pulled in at Tami's trailer off McIver Road, they'd finished their first beer. *I'm the Only One*, a Melissa Etheridge song, began on 103-ROX. Tami lowered the cool air and boosted the volume. Tapping the steering wheel in time and nodding to the lyrics, she handed Billie Jean another beer.

"That song always makes me think of stiletto heels and a bruised boyfriend," Billie Jean said as the two gathered the tanning essentials strewn near Tami's steps.

"Maybe that will be your next paper," Tami said. She and Billie Jean had met in May at Florence-Darlington Technical College. Holding a thin, tattered quilt suspended in one hand and a sweating beer can in the other, Billie Jean paused to consider Tami's suggestion. "That's a paper I could write," she said.

Their first English assignment had been a composition about an unforgettable experience. Tami described the time her water broke at the IGA. She titled her essay *Clean Up in Aisle Nine!*

"I never would have thought about that song that way," Tami

said. "First rule of writing, tell it like it ain't." She held open the trailer door for Billie Jean and pointed down the narrow hall. "There's a clean towel and shampoo above the toilet," she said.

Once when Billie Jean called to ask about their homework, Tami said she was examining her toddler's scalp. "What for?" Billie Jean asked.

"Three Sixes," Tami said.

But inside Tami's trailer now, Billie Jean didn't see a picture of the boy, not a toy, not a trace. Tami had made it all up.

After showering, Billie Jean sat loosely wrapped in a towel dreamily blow drying her hair and sipping her beer. "You can't imagine what we're in for tonight," Tami had said as they lay in the hot sun. "You can't begin to imagine." Tami waitressed at the Little Nashville Club most weekends. But George Miles, her bartender friend, asked if she'd moonlight at The Paradise Lounge the Saturday night before the race. It was the biggest bar night of the year. "We could use the help. It's just me and B.B," he'd said to her. "Bring a friend."

Billie Jean closed her eyes to the hum of the blow dryer at her ear, its soft warm air flowing down her back, over her shoulders. When she glanced up into the mirror Tami stood behind her half naked, her wet hair the color of butter and molasses. She smiled and tossed a T-shirt and a pair of red hot pants on the bed. "Wear the shirt inside out," Tami instructed. "Just do it," she said, smiling again, bringing one hand up to her hip, waiting. Then she turned and walked out.

In the small living area, Billie Jean checked her dangly earrings as Tami danced and sang. Their T-shirts spelled HOOTERS in the mirror. "We're two firecrackers wrapped in cellophane, ain't we," Tami said, moving to the music.

"Why are we wearing these inside out?" Billie Jean said. Their heads swayed to the music. "Because I said so," Tami said. Then she tossed her arm around Billie Jean's shoulder. "And because there's a shit load of money that's traveled all the way from Michigan and Ohio and New York just to jump in our pockets." Tami turned and pulled Billie Jean's hip to hers, setting her friend into motion with the music. "We're gonna rack up," Tami said.

"What'd I tell you?" Tami boasted. They crossed The Paradise Lounge lot like they owned it, a little deliberate extra in their runway strides. Tami announced the license plates they passed. "Tennessee,

Florida, Ohio, New York, New Jersey, New York. Come on, girl," she said laughing. "Rack 'em!"

When they stepped inside the bar, the red faces of sunburned strangers turned like scorecards at the Olympics. The happy hour Saturday race crowd was thinning, and B.B., Coach's wife, the shapely red-haired bartender, was clearing tables. Most of The Paradise Lounge regulars would be drinking at the Little Nashville Club. They liked being with their own on race weekends. The out-of-towners would soon line up at Skeet's Barbecue outside Darlington or Red Meat Rally in Florence for supper, but they'd be back. George Miles stood behind the bar. He spotted them.

George called to Tami. "I see you're dressed smart." He meant the owl faces that showed through the thin inside out T-shirts. From somewhere, a voice said, "Whooooooo that?" And another said, "Whooo cares what their names are, buy'em a round."

"How's it hangin'?" Tami said to George. She and Billie Jean were at the bar now.

"You too much," George said with a little laugh, pointing at their shirts. "You girls are too much. Hey, Billie Jean," he said with a tender nod. He spoke to Tami. "You want to stack the deck, don't you?" George opened the cash register, turned and smiled.

As he counted out twenty one-dollar bills, Billie Jean studied the room. She had waitressed at a fish place when she was in high school. But never in a bar, never more naked than not. Still, the afternoon's beers had been an elixir and a lubricant. Her flesh radiated summer heat and the mechanics of her limbs and hips felt fluid and graceful. She drew a deep, gentle breath and felt the caress of eyes like a soft, warm current.

Tami leaned way over the jukebox, feeding in the dollar bills. "We'll start with the Eagles," she said. "By ten, we'll be into Delbert McClinton. Midnight it's Hank William's Jr. and Lynyrd Skynyrd." She pressed lighted numbers and letters for the songs. "By one it's Mother's Finest, and at two it's AC/DC." She looked over at Billie Jean. "Everybody's gonna want a little AC/DC," she said. "Watch this." As *Peaceful Easy Feeling* began, she put her arm around Billie Jean's waist and pressed her hip against Billie Jean's, initiating the soft motion of their bodies.

"Damn, I need a drink," a voice behind them shouted. "Make that a round," called another.

"And they're off," Tami whispered with a smile.

By ten o'clock, race fans stood four-deep at the bar. George and B.B. marked drink orders on pads and Tami and Billie Jean made change at their tables. Music squalled and liquor flowed. The room was a blur of smiling red faces—clustered cheeks and foreheads like a mural of strawberries.

Delbert McClinton sang *Every Time I Roll the Dice* and Tami and Billie Jean held their trays high and stiff-armed anything that looked like a cheap feel.

"Tami!" George yelled. She turned. George pointed to his watch. She worked her way over to Billie Jean.

"And *my* question," Billie Jean said to the man smiling up at her, "is why are you talking to me but looking at my puppies?"

"Geeze!" the man said, turning to give his buddy a high-five. "If those puppies are for sale, I'll take the ones with the brown nose," the other man said. Both men had already begun reaching for their wallets.

"Come on," Tami shouted to Billie Jean over the noise and laughter. "To the bar."

George lined up shots of tequila. "Where's B.B.?" he shouted. The pretty redhead stood near the back wall, her serving tray drooped limp at her side, blankly staring at her husband. Coach sat in the near corner beside a guy wearing a turtleneck. George hit a switch, blinking the lights three times. B.B. saw the others waiting. George hit another switch shutting down the jukebox and The Georgia Satellites slurred to a stop. Every face turned toward the bar. The room was almost silent.

George looked out into the crowd and shouted, "What *time* is it, girls?" He raised his glass. B.B., Tami, and Billie Jean followed suit. Glasses everywhere in the room lifted in salute.

"It's *RACE* time!" George, B.B., and Tami shouted. The four threw back their liquor shots. George restarted the jukebox, race fans ordered another round, and together they all banked the first turn at 185 miles per hour.

At a quarter to the hour, The Wobblers sang *If You Ain't Here After What I'm Here After, You'll Be Here After I'm Gone* as George marched down the length of the bar waving a yellow flag, signaling all to order drinks for the next toast to the Southern 500. On the hour Billie Jean and Tami stood at attention beside George and B.B. Following tributes to The Paradise Lounge, Darlington—the heart and soul of NASCAR—to the love of sport and to all mankind, patrons raised their glasses and shouted, "It's *RACE* time!"

Men at every table pleaded to buy them beer or shooters. By midnight, Tami and Billie Jean were accepting offers. Their tight pockets overflowed with cash and they stuffed fistfuls of greenbacks into large plastic mustard jars behind the bar.

While B.B. and George poured drinks with both hands, Billie Jean surveyed the sea of smiling faces. Eruptions of laughter surged from first one table then another. Strangers gathered under the banner of their favorite driver, laced their arms around one another, tilted their heads and howled loudly and out of tune. Highball glasses and beer bottles rose in swells like whitecaps on a sea of happiness. Two women, one in a Dale Earnhardt T-shirt, the other in a Jeff Gordon T-shirt, embraced. Billie Jean thought: It's like a moment in a song when you hear just the right notes to make just the right chord, and the lyrics say what it is you're feeling in a way you always wished you could.

The whole room sang the chorus to the Wobblers' hit, *We Got Racin' Cars.*

"You are one beautiful thing," said the stranger in the turtleneck sitting at the bar beside Billie Jean. Billie Jean smiled, but her eyes followed Tami as she worked her tables.

"Look at *this*, youse guys," a man said. Tami was gliding toward them carrying their drinks on a tray. "There ain't a girl in all of Jersey that can walk like that there."

She was at the men's table now. "You got that right," Tami said to him.

"She's a knockout, ain't she," another man, Kurt, said. "That's my party girl."

Tami lowered her tray.

"Yeah, but I wonder how she holds her liquor," said the other man. All eyes were on Tami.

"By the ears," Tami said, not missing a beat, setting drinks down all around. After a stuttered moment of delayed synapse, Kurt's eyes flew open. His jaw dropped a notch. Then they shrieked in laughter. "If you'd give up them snakeskin cowboy boots to me," Tami said setting down the last man's drink, "I'd be a regular puss-in-boots." The men laughed so hard they had to turn sideways in their chairs. One threw his hand up as if about to testify. The one named Kurt drew a deep breath. You could see the laughing tears. The tip of his nose lit up like a purple bulb.

"What do they call you?" the man said, smiling at Tami, checking out her backside then looking over at his buddies.

"When they catch their breath," she said wedging a hand into her hip, "they call me *darlin'*." Kurt gasped for air like a swimmer going down, pushed his chair to the side, hugged his arms around his chest, and bowed his head. His torso bobbed like a cork on water.

"Damn, youse *killin'* me," another man said. He smiled at his friends and raised two twenties for the drinks. When Tami reached for the money, he pulled it back to his chest. "Say it again," he said. Tami cinched both hands to her hips. "Call me your darlin'," he said.

"You hard of hearing?" Tami said, snatching the money. The other men smiled.

"No, not *hod* of hearin', just *hod*, darlin'." He gave her his best puppy dog face. "Say it again—please?" He laid a ten on the table.

"Ol, *myyy,* darlin'," Tami said in her best Scarlett O'Hara, "that looks to me to be *folding* money?" She picked up the ten and the man laid down another. Patting her fingers to her lips, Tami faked a breathless swoon. "Oh, *my,* I think I'm feelin' faint, darlin'," she said in a high squeal. "Billie Jean? Oh, Billy Jeeean, darlin'?" she called.

Tami waved and Billie Jean coasted through the jammed bodies, the liquor in her veins like wind in a schooner's sails. She saw Tami's mock serious look. "Oh, sista, sista, darlin', you *must* see this. It's a damned *money* machine. Show sista, boys; show, huh." They all laid money on the table. "See?" she said, picking up the money. "Ain't that the damnedest thing?"

"Now *you* show'em," another man said. Their eyes clawed at the front of Tami and Billie Jean's T-shirts. Tami threw her arm around Billie Jean's neck, bringing her hand to rest near her breast. "You silly boys," Tami said. She gave the breast a deliberate, soft squeeze. Billie Jean flinched. Tami held her shoulder. "You Yankee boys got a lot to learn," Tami said, turning, taking Billie Jean's hand. "Fortunately for you," she said back over her shoulder, "y'all got all night to learn it." The men smiled, wagged their heads and exchanged looks of lust and wonder.

"*Tami—.*" Billie Jean said.

"Underneath our clothes, they know we're naked," Tami said. "Underneath their clothes, we know they're fools."

By one o'clock, George Miles had peeled back his eyelids, creating a spooky fisheye appearance. He danced like an Egyptian and sang about having friends in low places. He missed the yellow flag for the next race. But it didn't matter. NASCAR fans had begun to spin out and crash into the walls, and there wasn't a pit crew in America that could keep some of them on the track. During the vamp of AC/DC's *Highway To Hell*, George remembered the time, flicked the lights three times and killed the jukebox.

Billie Jean slid between the sweaty, tightly packed bodies, sinuously bathing in their flesh. Tami and fisheyed George were waiting behind the bar. But B.B., the other bartender, was at the far end, leaning forward in grave conversation. She glanced back at them, pleading. Billie Jean saw tears in B.B.'s eyes.

"He was my History teacher, that guy she's talking to," Billie Jean said.

"Her husband, Coach," Tami said. "He's a drunk. That's a walking caution flag you're looking at."

George flicked the lights for the next race.

Tami waited at the bar for drinks. Billie Jean tossed back a tequila shot then smiled. Tami thought: She looks like an actress. And at that moment, Billie Jean turned, giving Tami a smoky, sassy look, set her tray on the table and slowly breezed like an apparition across the room, feeling she could just keep going, sailing off into the sunset. The slow opening chords of an old Percy Sledge song soared from the jukebox and The Paradise Lounge dissolved into a movie, Billie Jean's movie. Now she was music and movement. Loose and free. Floating in the moment. A hot web of sensations tugged the damp T-shirt and gripped the tight red pants. As the primal music surged, she lifted her arms and closed her eyes, enticing that levitating feeling, inviting the music to have its way with her, to wash over her. She surrendered to the music. Tami danced in close, arms wide. The silent crowd parted then circled the two women as they swooned like underwater dancers.

Vapor, the guy in the turtleneck at the bar, turned to B.B.'s husband, Coach. "Don't think about it," he whispered. "Just watch'em dance." But Coach wasn't listening. Because he had spotted a man in the crowd. That man spoke to B.B. And when he did she lowered her eyes and smiled. Looking down into his drink, Coach whispered something Vapor didn't hear.

Other women joined Billie Jean and Tami, each dancing in her own imaginary column of light, trancelike: raised arms swaying in the music's soft tide of yearning, hips undulating, sometimes touching. Men and women closed the circled around them. No one spoke. There was only the music, the gentle sway of the crowd, their eyes half-shut in meditation or longing. Tami's hands cupped Billie Jean's waist.

44

A man with tears in his eyes threw the first punch.

At once, the contents of The Paradise Lounge began to spin. Tables erupted and glasses shattered. In a clumsy wild electric frenzy, small twisters of men ravaged and ransacked the room, their blurred fists flying herky-jerky. A hurling body hammered the jukebox. And where there had been music, a seething chorus of "motherfucker" detonated inside The Paradise Lounge as the spray and flow of blood, the nauseous splatter of flesh, and the caustic vomit of men spewed into the air like rank spit.

Whirling and shuttering like a man on fire, New Jersey Kurt jolted a man off his back, while another man gnashed and gouged, and another tasted the bloody flesh of a human ear. The spiraling, violent eddies raged out the door, into the parking lot.

Then the room was quiet, empty.

Billie Jean and Tami sat huddled behind the bar, staring up into the big mirror at the flashing blue lights outside. From the door George Miles called their names.

"What the *hell* happened?" Tami said, looking up at George. "Who's responsible for *this* shit?"

George looked down at the floor. "Coach," he whispered, nodding toward the far end of the bar. In a dark corner, Tami saw B.B. and the man who had been Billie Jean's History teacher. The two appeared to be slow dancing. Then she saw that B.B. was holding up her husband, who kept tilting side to side.

"Help me get him to the car," B.B. called.

Tami saw a swath of blood on the side of his face. She held one arm, B.B. the other. Outside, a city cop, one of his former players, looked at Coach, looked away, and turned his back. "You okay, B.B.?" the cop said softly. "B.B.?" She didn't answer. She didn't look at him.

Coach's wife opened the passenger door. He got in okay on his own. She turned and marched away without a word, without looking back. When Tami stepped up to shut the car door, Coach reached for her hand. "I know you," he said. Tami froze at the sound of his voice, then stepped back.

"No," she said. "I didn't go to your school. I'm from Hartsville."

"And you know me," he said. She couldn't look at him. She turned. "Wait," Coach said. "Please." She stopped. The night was dark and quiet. The blue lights from the police cruisers hovered around her like storm clouds. She turned. His eyes clear, bright. Not the eyes of a

45

drunk. "I can't tell her I love her enough," he said. "*You* know what I mean. You do. I know you do." Tami began backing away. "I can't," he said. His clear blue eyes held her. Tami couldn't take her eyes from his. "You know, all right." Then he turned and faced the windshield, his head high and steady, a perfect black silhouette.

George and Tami and Billie Jean were sitting at the bar. "Looks like a landfill, don't it?" Tami said.

"I'll drive you home," George said.

"One more shooter," Tami said. "A nightcap. Then we'll go party."

"What'll it be?" George said to Billie Jean. She didn't answer.

"Darlin'?" Tami said. Billie Jean turned away. The flashing blue lights from outside reflected in her eyes. Looking through the front window, the window Coach had driven his Mustang through a few months back, she watched as B.B. started the Honda and pulled away.

"No thanks," she said.

"That's just heat lightning," Tami said.

She and Billie Jean stood outside Tami's trailer looking up into the sky. Soft purple buds of light bloomed in the distant night sky. There was no thunder, no sound, not even crickets or frogs, only silence. "It never strikes," Tami said. George's red brake lights flashed at the end of the trailer park drive. She watched Billie Jean digging in her bag for car keys. "That's just heat lightning," Tami said again, shifting from side to side. She brought her fingers up to her mouth. She spoke in a whisper. "You ain't thinking about driving, are you?"

"I got to get home," Billie Jean said, looking down into her purse. "I feel like somebody beat me with a stick."

"Cops is swarming. You don't stand a chance this time of night." Tami looked at Billie Jean then looked up again at the distant lightning, then down at her feet. "Stay," she said softly.

"I gotta be going."

Tami hugged her arms to herself, nodded without looking up. "I'll get your stuff," she said.

Silence ringing in her ears, Billie Jean watched the display in the distant sky. Her tight shirt smelled of sweat, her damp hair of cigarette smoke. The old familiar weight of the end of a long night settled over her, the feeling of the tide emptying out, just going out and out of her.

"Look what *I* found!" Tami said brightly. Smiling, she held up two beers like trophies then sat on the top step to her trailer. "We showed 'em tonight, didn't we, Billie Jean? We rocked!"

"I gotta go."

"I know, I know," Tami said, patting the space on the step beside her. Tami was wearing her happy face again. "One beer. You and me. A little peaceful easy feeling, a soft landing." She patted the step. She popped open the two beers and Billie Jean sat beside her.

"What'd I tell you?" Tami said, passing a beer. A deep, gentle puff of distant thunder rolled overhead. "You and me. We were regular tag team champs. How much you reckon we pulled in?"

Billie Jean looked down then took a long drink.

"They cold, ain't they?" Tami said. A breeze lifted a tangle of Billie Jean's long black hair, swept it across her face. "I want to tell you a story," Tami whispered.

"What happened to your baby?" Billie Jean said, staring down into her beer. "The one you wrote your papers about. The one you told me about on the phone." She could feel Tami's eyes on her.

Billie Jean set down her beer, picked up her keys. Tami watched as she walked away. She was near her car. Tami looked up, speaking to the purple clouds. "Everybody's got a secret life, don't they, Billie Jean? Secret things that make them who they are."

Billie Jean opened the car door. The clock on the dash said 3:30.

"Don't they?" Tami said. Billie Jean turned.

"Yes," Billie Jean said. "They do."

Tami sat on the step with her knees pulled up tight, head down like a small child. "For a time, for a little while tonight, Billie Jean, everything was perfect, wasn't it? For a little while? Perfect."

"Yes. It was. It really was."

"Everybody's entitled, Billie Jean. You and me. We got to take ahold of these special moments. Cause they never last. Still, last or not, those times is what we live for, ain't they?"

"What is it you want, Tami?"

Tami looked up at the flickering pink and purple lights beyond the smoky bruised clouds. She drew a deep breath and lowered her eyes to the out yonder. Turning her head slowly from side to side, she spoke into the night. "What I want? What I want is what everybody wants, darlin'." Her lips formed something like a smile. She raised her beer in a toast. "Someone to crawl back to," she said.

Marion

We should have a *practice* honeymoon," LeAnn said into the full-length mirror. "A week at the beach would be perfect." She stood with her back to me, naked except for the new see through panties. "I want my marriage to be perfect this go-round." She lifted her chin, tossed back her shoulders, drew an expansive breath, held it, then cut her eyes my way. "Or not," she said. She turned, offering me a full-frontal. "Can you picture my tan lines, Marion?" I could. But July 4th is a big week in the wrecker business.

"Not a good time," I said. She swiveled this way and that, admiring her panty purchase, then ran her eyes up the length of me. "I'll talk to the mongoose about that," she said to the mirror, nodding a big uh-huh.

It was a bad one, I-95 between Santee and Florence. A long stretch of nothing. I know it well. My friend Zack calls it "Lullaby Lane," on account of the number of drivers who fall asleep at the wheel. He and his partner Brooke are EMS. Brooke and I were Biology Lab partners in high school.

Traffic had come to a stop, at least a mile long in the northbound. I took the emergency lane as the gawking motorists crept ahead. You could see the carnival lights, their colors like a canopy under the night sky. I parked in the median. Troopers, firetrucks. Jaws of life? Not. Outside their unit, Zack and Brooke waited for the traffic to clear. The deceased, a man and the only passenger Brooke claimed. But Zack took exception.

"The only thing for sure," Brooke said, "is that he or she was from Florida. The tags are about the only thing left."

"You don't even know that," Zack said. "You can't say that with total certainty. Could be a rental."

"Oh, Jesus," Brooke said to me wagging her head from side to side. She looked at Zack. "Screw you *and* your rental." She turned. "He's being his pissy self again," she said.

"You don't know," Zack said. He gestured and spoke to me like I was an umpire and he was contesting a call. "After seven years—."

"Would you just let it go?" Brooke said. "Jezzzzzzus."

"Hey," I said, looking from one to the other. "How y'all doin'? Lovely night, huh?"

"Okay," Zack said. He turned to Brooke. "Marion will be the judge. Here's the situation."

"Hey, Marion, sweetheart," Brooke said. "Do I get an invitation to your wedding?"

Zack said, "After seven years you think you know somebody. You save lives together, you share things you could never share, even with your wife. You think you know them."

"Don't buy this Zack-the-sentimental-act," she said to me. "He's workin' you."

"Okay," Zack said to her. "You tell it."

"There ain't no it."

"We get a call a couple of hours ago—."

"Here it comes," she said, "Zack, the Moral Majority."

"Hardee's drive-thru in Darlington," he said. "Man, mid-fifties, heart attack. He's got his food, his Diet Coke. He's taking a good hard pull on the straw in his soda. Before he can shift into drive, wham, hits him like a damned jackhammer. Then, listen to this shit, Marion. Brooke steals the guy's Hardee's Meal Deal order."

"I stole nothing."

"You sure as hell didn't pay for it."

"Regifting," Brooke said to me.

"You ate the guy's goddamn supper." Zack looked at me. "Who is this person, Marion?"

"Listen to this, Marion," she said. "Deal of a lifetime. You get a double cheeseburger, hot dog, fries, drink—and an apple pie for something like five bucks. Can't beat it for the price."

"She never had a second thought, Marion. Just tore the paper off that burger and went to town before she even had the siren on. I'm in the back, giving chest compressions. Damn," he said. He started down the embankment into the shadows. "I got to take a whiz."

Brooke called to him, "I offered to share." Then she turned, brought her eyes up to mine. "How about you? You having second thoughts?"

"About what?" I said.

"You know what. I know you, Marion, the length and width of every square inch of you. It's not that LeAnn's got your heart. It's your kidney she's got, ain't it?"

Two troopers directed traffic as the fire trucks and EMS pulled away and I winched up what was left of the BMW. I was northbound when my cell rang—again, but I didn't answer. LeAnn. Her third call. The first was to say, "Imagine Myrtle Beach, Marion. I'm naked, getting in the shower now." The second to say, "I'm out of the shower now, Marion, naked. I can hear the surf." This one to say, "I'm going to b-e-d now. There's going to be some practice honeymoon sex happening here. If you want to get in on it, you better hustle on over."

When we were in high school, there was this group of us. You know the story. Maybe you grew up watching the TV show *Happy Days* like we did. Each of us had our role. She and my football teammate Pete Hump were a couple. I was her go-to guy on the show. They'd fight, she'd come running to me, sometimes not fully dressed, etcetera. They married. She ran around. He drank. She ran around more. He drank more. Somewhere in there she was diagnosed with kidney disease. They divorced. She came running to me, sometimes not fully dressed. She needed a donor. I gave her a kidney.

It's dawn. The voice on the radio is Gregg Ervin's. Greg had been another cast member. We'd also played varsity baseball together.

"Call her back, Marion. Please. You know I have to log every call." Gregg was a 911 operator. "Tell her to stop calling me when you don't answer, okay?"

After the surgery, hers and mine, I bought and installed a slipper tub. The scar from the kidney operation made LeAnn feel quote-unquote less like a woman, she said.

Now I was washing her back, only half listening as she described our perfect beach trip, when she suddenly made a leap to the perfect wedding present. "A tanning bed!" she said.

"Not a good idea," I said. She slowly leaned forward and yanked the sponge from my hand. "You should change your name from Marion to No," she huffed, giving the sponge a quick dunk then scrubbing without apparent intent. "What you fail to accept, Marion, is that, like it or not, we're joined as one, you and me. Forever and always. We share a vital organ, you know. So why are you so controlling, Marion? Why?"

"Tanning bed?" I said, "We'd have to build on another room."

"I'm trying really hard to make this work, Marion. You've never had a failed marriage like I have. I want everything to be perfect this time around. Why won't you do your part? Why won't you meet me halfway?"

"Let's go out for a nice dinner," I said.

"You have this way of changing the subject," she said. "What we're talking about here is of *mutual* interest, a good, even tan?" She dunked, sloshing soapy water over the side. "I guess I could just lay out naked in the front yard and get a splotchy one. Would you like that, Marion?"

"The neighbors would."

She held up the sponge like an instructional aid. "Marriage is a mysterious thing," she said. "It changes people. It does. Sometimes just like that"—for effect she gave the sponge a hard fist. "Out of the blue," she said, "everything goes to shit." She looked at me like I was her puppy, one she loved but that had pissed on her new shoes. She brought her palm to my face. "Oh, Marion," LeAnn said. Slowly, deliberately, she stood, levitating like an offering. She raised her eyes to the up yonder and lifted her hands to the gods. "We can't imagine the peril that awaits." It was a line she'd picked up from a Romance novel. I should add that after the slipper tub failed to restore her feelings of femininity and positive self-image, I'd paid for breast implants. I watched as heaping bubbles descended over the mountains and through the woods. "This is a serious test. Myrtle Beach will tell the story," she said to Zeus.

"Let me take you out to dinner, LeAnn, something nice."

She handed me a towel. "Can't afford it. We may lose our hotel deposit." She was referring to Hedonism II, the Jamaican resort where she planned to spend our honeymoon.

"It's just a meal," I said.

"Not a good idea," she said mocking me. She turned her back for me to dry. "Thirty-five dollars? That's one Air Brush tanning session." I folded the towel over her shoulder and walked out.

My grandfather died when my dad was thirteen, and his death as you might expect was especially hard on Dad. The funeral director who buried Granddad took an interest in my father, helped him get through it. I think Dad wanted to do the same for others. My father worked at that funeral home. He didn't own it but he could do anything related to its services. When I was in high school, he tried to recruit me into the business. "Marion," he said, "if you can handle your money and your liquor, you'll be great at this." I thought he was nuts. Last thing I'd wanted was to work around dead people. Funny, how little we know about ourselves until after the fact.

Like my dad, I'm drawn to the service side of my job, what attracted him to the funeral business, pride in doing a job well, of following through at a time when loved ones couldn't.

I experience that connection when I spot my call on the side of the interstate, busted water pump, flashers blinking, a mother in tears, three small frightened daughters, sweat poring off them. I get everybody situated in the cool cab, load and secure the minivan and climb in. Mom squeezes against the passenger door with the middle child on her lap. The oldest girl holds the youngest in the tight space between us. Mom is mournful, thinking, What am I going to do?

It's quiet for a few miles. But the cab is cool. I make small talk about what might be wrong with the car, giving it the most positive spin without raising false hopes. I of course know the best, most honest mechanics. I offer what I can. Mom holds back her tears.

There is a moment when things could go either way, and in that space I feel the necessity to do something. I turn to the oldest little girl and in my best Donald Duck voice I ask her name and where she goes to school. The kids' eyes light up. They smile. Then I go through the same routine with the middle girl, only I speak in Goofy's voice. The kids laugh and Mom smiles. And then to the smallest girl, she's maybe three years old, I speak in the voice of Mickey Mouse. "And whose *mother* are you?" I say, and the bigger girls laugh and the baby girl tilts her head and points at her mom, and Mom laughs too.

The week of July 4th came and went. LeAnn reported experiencing lower back pain. The pain was unbearable. Menstrual pains, she said. Or worse. "Maybe my body has finally decided to reject a bad kidney," she said.

I was waiting to pay at Walgreens when Gregg Ervin, my high school friend, called to me. He looked sweaty but pale. Gregg had been starting pitcher when we were in high school. He didn't have great stuff, no speed or accuracy to speak of, but he always kept his composure, this interior balance. It was as if the previous pitch didn't exist once it had been delivered. He could throw one in the dirt or over the catcher's head or maybe the guy on first would steal second, and he'd say, "Give me the ball." He just never got flustered. And for that he won a lot of games. Taking 911 calls was the perfect job for him.

"Just here, you know, to pick up a prescription," he said, sounding a little too happy about his purchase. I thought he had more to say. When he didn't I moved on.

"Good to see you, Gregg," I said.

He shuffled up beside me as I made for the door.

Outside, he said, "We need to talk, Marion."

"It's LeAnn, isn't it?"

"Yes," he said.

"Then we ought to get in the cab where it's cool." He hesitated, looked all around like there should be an exit sign. "We'll burn up out here," I said.

I directed two of the cool air vents to Gregg. "She called you again."

"That's the problem, Marion."

"I appreciate you letting me know, Gregg. I'll take care of it."

"I don't know if you can," he said. Not what I expected to hear. He wiped his face and stared into the windshield. "The only thing I'm good at is logistics, Marion. I'm just a link in the chain, you know? I gave her my cell number so that her calls wouldn't show up at work."

"The calls are personal," I said.

"Damage control, that's what I do, Marion. I didn't just run into you by accident. I followed you in. Truth be known, at the time I thought I could help save y'all's relationship."

His eyes told the story. "She's in love with you, isn't she, Gregg?" I'd seen those eyes before, looking back at me in the mirror. "I appreciate your manning up," I said. I offered him my hand. He took it. We both looked out the windshield, out at the heat waves dancing above the asphalt. Then he reached for the door handle. "You all right?" I said. I indicated the white prescription bag.

"I'm fine," he said.

I go to The Paradise Lounge when I need to be alone. Or when I need to be with my friends. I go there most often when I find myself between those two conditions. It's a busy Friday night, a good time to be alone surrounded by others. George Miles, the bartender, picks up my glass and fills it with ice and pours a healthy bourbon. Before he can deliver it, I hear Zack call my name from across the room. He and Brooke are several drinks ahead of me.

"Come 'ere, quick," Zack called. "I need a steady hand." Brooke pulled out a chair beside her. Zack slid his camera across the table.

"Take her picture," he commanded.

"Not now," Brooke said. "I'll need a minute to take my clothes off."

"You wish," Zack said. "Hey, George!" he shouted. "Bring Marion a drink, on me." George looked at me and I signaled no. "Listen to this," Zack said. "I need Brooke's picture."

"I once was lost," Brooke said. She turned to me. "But now I'm found."

"No, no, no," Zack said. "An APB, Marion, an APB. Haven't you heard?"

"No," I said. Brooke rested her hand on my thigh.

"Look at her," Zack said.

"Yes, do," Brooke said.

"She says that she was a Daisy Scout. You be the judge, Marion. Do you believe that claim?"

"Yes," I said.

"Good," he said. "Me, too."

"Are they arresting Girl Scouts?" I said.

"That's good, Marion. You hit the nail on the head." He raised his hand and we did a soft high-five. "That's fucking good."

"You don't know where this is going, do you?" Brooke said.

"Don't have the foggiest," I said.

"Someone or someones," Zack lifted his glass, held it suspended for an accusatory second then drank. "Someone with insider knowledge." He stopped abruptly. "I forgot to tell you this part, Marion, a very important piece of evidence. Guess who had the night off last night." He offered Brooke a toast. "Miss Daisy Chain here, that's who. Take her mugshot, Marion."

Brooke said, "Zack is referring to a reported larceny in Charlotte."

"Last night, I remind you," Zack said. "A warehouse." I looked from Zack to Brooke to Zack. "How well do you know her, Marion?" Brooke squeezed my thigh.

"Since high school," I said, prompting another squeeze.

"Me, I know everything about her," he said. "Seven years, you come to know everything. I even know what Girl Scout cookies she eats, not that she's very particular about what she puts in her mouth." Another squeeze, this one sustained. "Did I tell you she stole this dead guy's Meal Deal? And ate it?" He nodded disapproval. "That's vile Brooke. Vile."

"You were saying?" Brooke said. Her smile was meant for me.

"So the warehouse thieves. They break into a warehouse, see, one filled with Girl Scout cookies. Only get this: They only steal the Thin Mints and Peanut Butter Patties. Ask her, Marion, ask her which cookies she eats. Take a picture of this thief while I take a whiz."

Brooke and I watch as Zack negotiates the crowd. Then she turns to me. "Everything about you makes me want to be bad," she says. Whatever I'm supposed to say, I don't say it. She takes her hand from my thigh. "If I was you," she said. "I'd get my kidney back. I'd sue."

I know right many of the troopers by first name. At the Highway 52 slash I-95 interchange I see blue lights, my buddy Lee directing traffic. We may never know what really happened there. Neglect and carelessness generally determine who will be at fault. But often it's complicated. The trooper might interview the drivers and witnesses who give conflicting stories. The adjusters may assign a portion of blame to the parties involved. Some of the most important evidence may not be allowed in the courtroom. Even when negligence is defined as actions that fail the tests of caution and responsibility, fault can be impossible to determine. Sometimes it's not what we do but what we fail to do.

In the wrecker business, you soon learn not to spend too much time thinking about what can't be known. You try to avoid the moment of impact, the last breath. The explicit evidence splattered right in front of you. As for what isn't there, most of us have no words. The most important thing, as my father would say, is to follow through when others can't. Safety, he said, is a lie we have to tell ourselves. And when that lie is laid bare we all need some degree of human protection. He taught me that the hardest thing is helping others find a voice to say goodbye.

I already know the shape our conversation will take, LeAnn's and mine. Its curves, caution lights and detours. I hear it playing out. I even hear the sounds of our voices in my head. You know, the he said slash she said back and forth. The pauses packed with meaning, the double meanings and reversals. That moment of silence when things could go either way. Maybe this ability to project events serves as a kind of safety device, like air bags.

"And I'm okay with that," I say.

What she hears is the voice of her go-to guy.

But that voice isn't mine.

Vapor

Mom and I were playing snake. In the dark. On the porch steps. Taking turns.

She wore a thin red skirt.

Nobody was saying anything. Her eyes were far away, lost. Out back Dad worked in his shop inventing a revolutionary new gas grill that would soon explode, blowing him into tiny red specks. Before he could stand trial for murder.

Mom and I sat side by side in the shadows, as if I wasn't there.

In the distance, the lights from the church softball field produced a bright nuclear glow above the tall green corn, its motionless leaves hanging like daggers. On the opposite horizon, the full moon sat bright and red as a giant ember.

She lifted and slowly rotated her glass, its ice like white jelly-beans. As she slowly panned the stretch of highway in one direction then the other the red moonlight set her eyes ablaze. Her breath smelled of green pine needles.

The snake lay waiting.

The night's first breeze stirred. "Something's up," I said.

She tucked her skirt between her knees and reached down to the brick step, lifted the fishing line, laid it in my palm.

"That's enough of that," she said. She stood and started inside to make herself another liquor drink.

"Why?" I said. From over the horizon, the distant roar of softball fans passed overhead like a tender amen on the summer breeze.

She let the screen door slam behind her and sang the words to *Just My Imagination*.

Headlights flared up from the direction of the game. I wrapped the clear twenty-pound test filament around my hand and formed a fist, then hunched on the porch step like a sprinter at the starting line.

"Mama? Mama!" I shouted.

I pulled the line tight, held it low. The headlights blinked bright, making it impossible for me to judge the car's speed. Drawing a deep breath, I slowly worked the line. Pull, pause. Pull, pause. Pull—. The black asphalt lit up. Our snake slithered across. But I'd been too quick in my delivery. The snake was already in the middle of the other lane. The driver never had a chance.

"Missed that one by a mile," Mom said through the screen behind me. Like she was talking to herself.

I dropped the fishing line and hustled out to the road. It was a fine snake, one with lots of action. Thick and black like a water moccasin. Mom had made it from a bicycle inner tube. She'd cut the tube in half, like a big C, then folded back the bottom half at the center and stapled it in the middle to make an S. Folded the tip on one end to make a V, meaning poisonous, and stapled on the fishing line. We were waiting for the softball game to end, for the cars to come speeding by. I lifted our black rubber snake, positioned it in the grass on the far side of the road and ran back to the porch where Mom sat. I was trying hard not to think about anything.

"Why?" I whispered. At first I didn't believe she'd heard me. Her eyes looked out farther than they could see, then slowly ascended to the blood red moon as she drank.

The fun of playing snake was seeing drivers risk their lives to squash half a rubber inner tube they imagined to be a snake. They'd swerve, lock up their brakes, lay their lives on the line for that satisfaction. The evening's first attempt had proven as much when the Cro-Magnon driver of an empty pulpwood truck slammed his brakes so hard the trailer tires bounced and smoked. He pulled over onto the shoulder and waddled back the forty yards axe in hand. When he looked up at us, Mom and I just waved and waved, smiling like lunatics on a Christmas parade float. "Snake," he called to us. We nodded in agreement. Guy must have spent ten minutes stomping up one side of the ditch bank then down the other side, axe raised and ready, doing his Paul Bunyan routine while the object of his fear and wrath lay flat and lifeless under my mom's feet. As he drove away, she raised her hand to high-five, threw back her drink, and smiled. "Another stupid-fat-fuck in a big-ol' truck," she sang in a hick voice, slowly shaking her head from side to side like it was sad, sad news.

I turned away. Sometimes I couldn't bear looking at her.

Earlier in the day I'd watched from the tall corn as she climbed behind the wheel of the man's truck. The air conditioning guy rounded the corner of the house holding his toolbox. She smiled. I just stood there, eyes wide, and watched. Her smile was both happy and mean.

He opened the door to the big truck. She lay back on the seat and lifted her red skirt. I nearly vomited. That taste was in my mouth. I whispered a prayer in fear that she was leaving Dad and me. Once, Dad let me wear his welding helmet and laughed when I spoke in my best Darth Vader voice.

While she was putting supper on the table, I stood at the window looking into his shop at the very back of the yard. Welding sparks flew diving past its open door like fiery minnows. He told me not to look, that it would blind me.

Our family sat in silence. I know the sound of a knife or a fork on a plate is a small sound, but as we ate our supper, I felt I was in the middle of a sword fight. I couldn't stand it another second.

"There's something dead around here," I said.

My father looked at her. "Yes," he said. He pushed his plate away and walked outside to his shop.

My mother gave me a thin-lipped smile and pulled her shoulders up high and tight like a bat tucking its wings. "Let's play snake," she said.

We waited. The blood had drained from the moon. It was pink and yellow, higher now, and you could see its dimples. Past the tall corn in the other direction, the softball field lights were brighter, sharper— the stars shimmied. Every few minutes waves of cheers, puffs of cushioned air, were carried toward us on the summer night's breeze.

"A close one," I said.

"Just your imagination," she whispered into the darkness. We waited.

For obvious reasons, we never turned on the light above the porch steps when we played snake. We spoke in whispers, as if we sat together in a tiny closet. With the door closed. Her face was a shadow. Mine a shadow. Alone with our dark fascination.

I'd watched as the man's brown hands stroked her white hips. Then I sat in the middle of the corn row with my back to it, listening to her wordless cries.

Another soft wave of cheers passed overhead.

"I'm going back to Dad's shop," I said.

"No," she said, her fingers cuffing my thigh, holding me in place. "Look," she said. "Game's over." A column of headlights raced up the highway. "Here," she said, quickly wrapping the fishing line around my open hand. "You go first. Do it, big boy," she said. "Do it good."

I gave the string a series of little jerks.

"Perfect," she whispered. "Feel that? Feels *good*, don't it?"

The first car swerved across the centerline, followed closely by a second and a third. We heard a tire leave the highway, then spin back on. The rubber snake bubbled on the asphalt like beads of black water on a griddle. A chain of red brake lights flew by.

"*Yes!*" she said. She stood and carried her empty glass inside. "Go set us up," she said through the screen. "Don't get run over," she called over her shoulder.

Not knowing where the snake had landed, I followed the clear line into the darkness, allowing it to run freely through my fingers like the eyes of a fishing rod. The line descended into the shallow ditch. I knelt in the wet grass and reached blindly. My fingers found it. Then peering down into the blackness I suddenly envisioned a real cottonmouth, thick, black, eyes like tiny flares. Cocked and ready. Its wide mouth foaming with venom, red sparks leaping from its twitching tongue. A pain like electricity shot up my arm. I snatched back my hand and felt the blood throb in my throat. I shot to my feet and jerked, heaving up our snake: A blinding white wall of light rocked me. The blare of the car's horn passed through my chest, and a blast of hot air blew back my hair, the driver's slurred curse a wailing smear of sound. My arms flew up. Dark specks like dust motes floated before me. I dropped my hands from my eyes and watched as the night sucked the car's red taillights into blackness.

Then all was quiet. Dark. The stars faded in. My insides were shaking, my skin tingling. I crossed the road and slid the snake into the thick wet grass on the other side, wiped my hand against my shirt and ran to the porch.

Mom was standing in silhouette at the open screen door looking down at me, one hand at her hip. The end table lamp was lit up behind her. Behind me, another line of cars from the game flew by.

"Good boy," she said, taking her seat on the dark brick step before slowly lifting her glass. I handed her the fishing line, but I didn't sit.

"Your turn," I said. "I'm going to check on Dad."

"No, no," she said quickly, a tiny spray of pine needles showering each word. She patted the space beside her. "Go again. You did good. Go again." She held up the line for me to see. I glanced down at her face, but I couldn't look at her. "Shut out the light. Then sit. Sit," she said in that musical voice again, reaching for my hand. Her fingers smelled of perfume or soap.

When I reached for the line, she held my shoulder and hugged me close against the side of her damp, warm breast. "That's my boy," she said. "That's my champion snake boy."

Headlights formed a pack. We heard their far-off engines. I gave the line a tug. Her hand covered mine and brought it against her. Held it there. "No," she whispered. "Too fast." The pack blew by. She held my hand.

"A-ha!" she said, looking across to the softball field. "Lights out," she announced. Another cluster of traffic whizzed by. "We'll get some singles now," she said, "good ones." She held my knee. "United we stand," she said. "Divided they fall." Her hand was damp and warm.

"I'll see about Dad now," I said.

"No. All yours," she said. I couldn't look at her. She bumped her shoulder against mine. Smiling, she motioned toward the single set of headlights. "Take her," she said. Her eyes were eager, hungry, waiting. "Now," she said. My hand wouldn't move. "Do it," she commanded. I pulled. Too late. The driver hadn't seen the snake. Cruised by. "That's strike two," she said. "Go set him up for your mom."

I jumped the ditch on my return and started across the wet lawn. In the sky above the roof, the reflection of my father's rhythmic welding bloomed in the high pink clouds like heat lightning.

She leaned forward on the step, elbows on her knees, rubbing her hands as if she were making a wish. "I got a feelin'," she sang. She lifted her glass and sipped. "I think you and me could put this on TV," she said, looking off into the darkness. "A cross between a reality show and a game show. We'd get rich. We'd live in Hollywood." Behind her I saw headlights above the tall corn. The wind had picked up, and the stalks danced and clapped like flailing ghosts. You could smell the ripe corn juice.

"Just go," I whispered. The headlights were close.

"Why? Is it my turn?" The car passed with a quiet unfolding. "Missed it," she said to herself. "We're a team, you and me big boy, the two of us," she lifted her glass. "You and me," she drank. "We'll get rich. What would you call it?"

I hadn't felt my insides knotting up. But suddenly I tasted vomit at the back of my throat.

"You get to name our TV show," she said, like she was doing me a favor.

"Living with Snakes," I said.

She lifted her glass again, tilted back her head, eyes closed, then nodded approvingly. "That's *goood,*" she said.

Even before we saw the headlights above the tall corn, we heard the car's engine winding up. She leaned forward, holding the fisted line between her open knees. "Come to Mama," she whispered. "Simply irresistible." The pitch of the engine rose to a yearning whine and the flickering headlights raced toward us above the tall flailing stalks of sweet corn. "Just your imagination," she whispered, pumping her fist back and forth, back and forth, between her legs. "Like *this.*"

The sound of burning rubber trailed behind the streak of white light, followed by a frozen silence that hung suspended in the air before the explosion of glass and metal. I heard the car tumbling, felt it like blows to my chest. Then nothing.

We were on our feet, hands raised to fend off the invisible. "Oh, oh," she cried taking two steps forward before collapsing to her knees.

Then I was running. I glanced back. She was on all fours. "Help me," she cried. "Help me." Her hands were kneading the grass in front of her, feeling for the fishing line. "Snake!" she screamed, "Snake!"

Half-a-football field ahead, moonlight broke through the dirty gray cloud of dust that churned above the crumpled, smoking metal and broken glass. The smell of burnt rubber, raw upturned dirt, black and rich, sweet corn and gasoline hung in the air. My legs wouldn't stop pumping. Steam and smoke poured like foam from the wide, gaping hood of the car, its interior glowing like a red lantern. "Don't look, Don't look," I whispered. My body was not my own. Mother's wordless cries were like a hot breath at my ear. "Don't look," I said. Elbows and feet pounding like pistons. I forced my eyes down to the black asphalt.

Dust descended like a gray veil. Searing flames reflected in my red eyes. I smelled burning flesh.

Don't look, I thought. Don't look.

But I couldn't stop myself. And even now as I close my eyes, I see my smiling father beside his new revolutionary gas grill. "Watch this," he says.

Russ

By the time I'd made the two-hour drive to their Charleston apartment, to Chloe and Pete's little love nest, my hands were so swollen I had to kick in the door. I'd planned to jimmy it open. A jimmied door suggests a crime of convenience. A kicked-in door signals a crime of passion.

I didn't know what I would do when I found Chloe, but I knew I'd better do whatever I could to cover up whatever it was I was about to do. Still, because my hands were so swollen, I couldn't hold the screwdriver. I kicked in the door.

When the blue lights appeared twenty minutes later, I was sitting in my truck—make that Pete's truck, Pete Hump's Plumbing #2—nursing my puffy, bloody knuckles, feeling numb and empty inside. Discovering that your wife is doing the dirty with your boss, a guy you've known since middle school, takes something out of you. To top things off, the cops showing up like they did meant that Pete had set me up, that he was still alive, that the beating he'd taken hadn't been beating enough. What I'd left and what I'd found weren't what I thought they'd be. I thought I'd left Pete dead, and I thought I'd find Chloe in an apologetic mood.

I watched the two blue uniforms enter the dark apartment building. Inside, the cops would see what I'd seen, soiled sheets in an otherwise empty apartment, nothing missing or turned upside down. Only their eyes wouldn't well up with tears and their blood wouldn't boil. They'd see a scene of passion, but they wouldn't see a crime. That would have to wait.

I started the engine, dropped the transmission into D, and eased away from the curb. Heading west out of Charleston onto I-26, I reached for the two-way radio, the one connected to Pete Hump's #1.

"I have just two things to say," I said into the mike. "First, I love you, Chloe, and I want you back. And second, I hate your guts, Pete, and I'm gonna rip off your head and shit down your throat. Over?" I set the mike on the floor and felt under the seat for a roll of duct tape. Pete's voice came back.

"Remember these words?" he said. "A choir of naked peasant women. Slowly dancing. In a giant tent. In a field. Over?"

I tore off a strip of duct tape and pressed it over the key-up button, keeping the channel open on this end, and reached for my favorite Lynyrd Skynyrd CD, the live one from the Fox Theatre in Atlanta. Sure, Pete could cut me off at the other end, but every time he switched on that radio, which he couldn't resist, I'd be there. Me and the Skynyrd boys. I set the mike near the stereo speaker, punched up *Saturday Night Special* and pumped up the volume.

When I reached the city limits of Darlington, the sky had the pink light you see at dawn in the South in the summer. It cracks open the night, making way for somebody's first day, somebody's last. Still, the I-95 billboard lights above the plumbing shop advertisement were so bright the sign seemed to float in the dim sky. Its words, Pete Hump's Heat Pumps, spoke of something mocking, something vile.

I took the Pocket Road exit. A change of clothes, a Smith & Wesson .357 and a bottle of bourbon were the only things I'd need. I eased up the long path to my hunting cabin, left the engine idling and Skynyrd playing. My hunting clothes, minus the jacket, were where I'd left them, but my pistol was gone, which meant only one thing. Pete had it.

Outside, I started for the truck. Columns of sunlight suddenly shot from behind the clouds and through the pines, spraying glitter over Black Creek, flickering upon the little island where Chloe sunbathed. The specks bright, the island empty.

My boys sang *Gimme Three Steps*. I shifted into reverse and thought of what Pete had said over the radio about the naked peasant choir in the tent in the field. He was desperate.

Pete forgets I know Chloe better than he does, that I've lived with her, cooked and cleaned and waited on her hand and foot, pleaded like a beggar. Chloe gets her way, and I know that way better than Pete does. So, while Pete thinks that he's gonna be messing with my mind, that he'll be clever and outthink and outsmart me, he will at the same time be like a bird dog on a covey of quail. And that scent is my wife's. He thinks he's making his own decisions, like that bird dog thinks he's making his. Truth is, he has no choice but to follow the path that's been laid out in front of him. And neither do I. But soon he's gonna develop a pain in his nose that I didn't put there, the one that comes from having

Chloe lead you around. And soon after that, he'll be a dead man.

I reached down and lowered the volume on the CD player. Picked up the mike with my sore, swollen hand.

"Trashy Pete. In a hole. In a field. Doing the dance," I said. "Chloe, I still want you back." Then I turned up the volume for the long guitar solo at the end of *Free Bird*.

Just because he once saved my life, Pete thinks I might allow him his. I'd been a dead man, seen the light on the near-death side, been given a peek over the edge, hovered above the scene, watched from up there as Pete hammered my lifeless heart until it fired up again.

At the moment I reentered life on earth, I opened my eyes and Pete and I exchanged an ESP vision of that moment.

"Choir," I whispered.

"Naked peasant women," he said.

"In a tent," I said.

"In a field," he said.

But that gave him no right. No right at all.

To him, the slow dancing choir was living evidence of the force and power of mystery, another way of saying that destiny ruled the direction life takes. In a kind of evangelical call and response, we'd said as much on that faithful day.

That shared visionary experience had been our secret connection, our secret code, our covenant. Our way of making sense of the things we couldn't understand, the unforeseen and unexplainable. That private encounter from the other side became our key to accepting mysteries on this side. A kind of acceptance that others acquired only from history.

And with good reason. Coach and B.B.'s love had been testament to our shared vision, theirs a covenant sanctified by the words he said to Pete and me on their wedding day: "You can't imagine it," Coach said, smiling, happy tears in his eyes. "After it happens, you know it had to be."

You can't imagine it, but afterwards you think you should've seen it coming. Love. Death. Coach and B.B. Chloe and Pete.

Now Pete was trying to tie the strings of infidelity into a delusional knot, saying to me that he and Chloe were like history or one of those things that a man can't find words to say, a way of describing events and feelings that can't be explained.

A way of saying it wasn't his fault.

But I was in no mood to admit that he could be right, to own up to what I knew about Chloe, or to surrender to the knowledge that Pete never had a chance after Chloe applied her will. No mood at all.

On this side of Columbia, I gassed up at the Pilot Truck Stop. When I opened my wallet for the Pete Hump's Plumbing credit card, I saw my wife's picture.

Chloe. Three thousand miles away in Hollywood, women were spending a fortune on plastic surgery, personal trainers, acting teachers, and therapists just to master a cheap imitation of Chloe's natural walk. Children stared at her on the street. Every bi-curious woman in town dreamed secretly of Chloe, every man measured his loss in not having her, and both men and women from all walks of small town life described her as drop-dead gorgeous. In Charleston or Savannah or even Atlanta, strangers asked her if she was a movie star. None of this was lost on Chloe, who accepted her charms like fashion accessories, or the way Fred Benton, who was born with two thumbs on one hand and who owned a three-balled tom cat, couldn't imagine that hand with only one thumb or his cat with two nuts. She had come to feel—for every good reason—that she was destined for something else, something better. Something that didn't include me.

The skinny woman working the drive-thru near Spartanburg handed back change. "That's Skynyrd," she said, wagging her head to the music and stuffing my fries into the McDonald's bag. "I remember them," she said.

"This song?" I said. I set the bag on the seat beside me and received my coffee.

"No," she said. "The plane crash."

"Me, too," I said.

Crossing the French Broad River in North Carolina, the Van Zant boys and I wailed the words to *Tuesday's Gone*. I lowered the volume and picked up the mike.

"Remember these words," I said. "*The Porter Wagner Show*. Special song request: *Act Naturally*. Save room on the roller coaster for me, okay, buddy?" I grinned to myself. That Porter Wagner part would put the spook in Pete. He'd realize I knew where the two lovebirds were headed. He'd know I wasn't too far behind. Pete's eyes would fly open in that Nicholas Cage way and his sphincter would shut so tight you couldn't hammer a twenty-penny nail up there.

He would then explain to Chloe the necessity to change plans. She'd turn to him and part her sumptuous lips. Pete would stop mid-sentence and Pete Hump's truck #1 would become something like a heat-seeking missile, destination: Dollywood.

Best I could figure, Pete had three hours on me. They could be near Pigeon Forge by now.

Up ahead, the Blue Ridge Mountains ascended. The air became thin and cool and the high midday clouds looked like a breath of cold air. I thought about what it must be like up there, looking down. And soon I was thinking about Skynyrd peeking out the tiny windows of that plane, thinking about their next show in Baton Rouge, or the other one they'd never play at Madison Square Garden, maybe feeling a new song working its way through their excited hearts, or maybe thinking about loved ones back home in Jacksonville. Knowing not where they would come down. Knowing not that what they were about to lose would be lost forever. Unaware that a softly swaying choir of naked peasant women in a giant tent, in an open field, might, when all was said and done, be as good as it gets. I punched up track #3, *Searching*.

There is no easy road to Dollywood, only sharp steep turns, tunnels that require headlights, warnings to look out for rock slides. A boulder descends from nowhere, squashes you like a bug.

Chloe tried to tell me. Sometimes, she said, you have to get close to certain people, places or things to know who you are and where you belong. You search those things out. At Dollywood she'd take in the mountain air and believe again that all things are possible, that she'd been put together the way she was, like Dolly Parton, for a reason. That she was meant to be somebody.

"I work on cars," I said to the two slope-headed kids gawking at my cut, swollen hands. We were waiting in line at the entrance to the theme park. "Race cars," I said. "I'm a mechanic." Their mother, a large woman dressed in an orange and green print, gave me a slack-jaw look and gathered her two toads against her tractor tire hips.

"No you ain't," the boy said.

Not wanting to drift too far from the main exit, I bought ice cream and took up position near Adventures in Imagination. Spotting them wouldn't be a problem. The crowd would part for Chloe. Pete would be trailing close behind. Before I finished my ice cream two park attendants began giving me the fish eye, like I was an escaped convict or a pervert. One spoke into his walkie-talkie and nodded to the other.

They turned their eyes on me.

I drifted over to Jukebox Junction. I stood zombielike staring at the flow of people. Thinking about my years with Chloe.

I considered the thing that deep down I already knew. I closed my eyes. When I opened them, I was suddenly swept up in a tide of tourists, forced down a bending, twisting course like a tiny particle in a blood vessel, not knowing where or why. I lost my bearing. Finally I stood alone, looking up at the brilliantly painted sign of the Blazing Fury roller coaster, at the flames, and hearing the words of *I Ain't The One* playing in my head.

A thick gray haze lay like a soft fluffy blanket over the mountains, and way back the dying pink sunlight condensed into a dark red hue. With Knoxville in my rearview mirror, I suddenly felt tired, top to bottom, through and through. But I pressed the gas. My destination, our destination, mine, Chloe's, Pete's was Graceland, the second stop on Chloe's quest. But I couldn't help feeling that I was running from, not running to.

Around midnight I pulled into the first rest stop west of Nashville. Twenty-four hours earlier I'd stood in the ocean air amidst the sinful sweat of a strange apartment in Charleston and looked down on the crumpled sheets of two lovers. Now, in the middle of Tennessee, I experienced the jarring feeling of time slamming up against time, of being in places unconnected at the same moment. I felt like a stranger in a foreign country.

I shut off the engine. The sudden quiet rang in my ears.

At the concession shelter, I bought two soft drinks, two packs of peanut butter crackers and two candy bars. At a picnic table away from the lights, I ate the crackers and the candy bars, downed one of the sodas. I watched the I-40 traffic come and go. Heard the toilets flush. Pete and Chloe were in some motel. In the morning, a small dark woman from a foreign country would come into their room, switch on the TV and strip the bed like nothing had happened there.

Back in the truck, I opened the second soda, drank most of it then refilled the can with bourbon. I sipped slowly, feeling the muscles in my neck and back unknot. Overhead, moths and bugs swarmed and circled the blue halogen street light. I pondered what music called them to dance like that. I drank.

Then I recalled our fishing trip after high school graduation, the year Coach took us to the state football championship. We'd spent most of the day drinking beer and driving up to Lake Mattamuskeet in North Carolina. Along the way, Pete told me about his brilliant idea for night fishing.

It was late afternoon when we set up camp. Just before dark we unloaded the boat and cruised about a mile across the water to where Pete said the biggest bass would be. He set a lit lantern on a cypress stump and we headed back.

That was his bright idea.

About midnight, we puttered back across the shallow lake with our cachet of Rebels, Devil's Horses, hoola-poppers, pet spoons, and plastic worms. I shut off the engine and we glided silently to within casting distance of the lantern. The water around the lighted cypress churned like a washing machine. "I told you," Pete said. The bugs had come to feast on the light. The bass had come to feast on the bugs. "We're gonna slay 'em," he said. We cast our lures. We both hooked monsters. Pete handed me his rod and reached for the flashlight and the net.

The water moccasins had come to feast on the bass.

The water was thick and alive with them. We cut our lines. I pulled up anchor. Pete hit the starter on the motor. Nothing. We had only one paddle.

"Can't just sit here," Pete said. "If we drift, they'll soon be in the boat. This is my fault." He slid over the side, into that night, into that dark, infested, clammy water, taking only a length of the anchor rope. "You stay in the boat," he said, then turned and pulled. There was no moon. No way of knowing exactly how far from land we were. No way of knowing what the next step meant. No way of seeing it coming.

I was too afraid to move. Too afraid not to. I watched the muscles in Pete's shoulders. My friend in the dark lake of serpents. He trudged through the muck. I slid off the boat into the black water and pushed.

Back at camp we threw our arms around one another, then sat before the fire like victorious warriors, drinking without talking, looking up one to the other from time to time, teammates, state football champions.

Tapping at the window woke me. The woman wore a hat like a forest ranger's.

"You can't sleep here," she said. "Overnight parking isn't allowed. But you sure looked like you could use some."

I got coffee from the machine and headed west for Memphis, final destination—for all of us—Graceland.

I'd be closing in on Pete and Chloe, driving while they slept. Or whatever. I shut off the CD player and counted the mile markers. For the first time since discovering that Pete was still alive and on the run with Chloe, I tried to picture just what I'd do when I got my hands on him.

My mind's eye carried me only as far as the gates of Graceland. There I'd find Pete, alone. Chloe was a divining rod seeking water, a seer awaiting a sign. With a quiet command, she'd leave him solitary and stunned and enter the big house alone, there to breathe air of the King. Floating like a specter from room to room, unaware of the long adoring looks from strangers or their astonished whispers, Chloe would feel the rapture, signifying her rightful place among the likes of Dolly Parton, Ava Gardner and Marilyn Monroe.

Pete would never see it coming. Then he would see me.

It wouldn't be the first crash landing at Graceland. With a .38 derringer on the dash of his Lincoln Continental and a bottle of champagne in hand, Jerry Lee Lewis had buried the nose of his Lincoln into the musical notes of that gate. Jerry Lee, *The Killer*. I'd be in good company. Pete would be standing there awaiting he'd know not what. When he saw me, his face would do that twisted up, hurts-so-good, upside-down smiling Nick Cage thing. I would draw back my aching fist as I had two nights before.

But that's where my imagination stopped. Only history would reveal what happened next. I had no idea.

As I neared its city limits, Memphis reached out and pulled me in. I looked for signs to Graceland, for the Elvis Presley Boulevard exit. I turned up the music and watched the faces of people as they zoomed by, tapped my foot and pretended I was one of them. I began to feel a kind of growing excitement. It wasn't happiness, but it was a happy feeling, a feeling that something big was about to happen, that something I couldn't see coming was coming right at me. The feeling was undeniable, turbocharged, like burying the speedometer needle at 130 miles an hour, then shutting off the headlights. I wanted to rush out to meet that feeling, whatever it was, whatever the consequences. I was headed for a head-on, I just didn't know with what. Everything was about to change, seemed like, as Ronnie, Live in Atlanta, sang *The Needle And The Spoon*. I bowed my head, shut my eyes, raised my hand and said, "Come and get me, Lord."

At that very moment Van Zant shouted that he was *going down to Memphis town*. Him and me.

I lifted my head and opened my eyes. Some force, a power not my own, steered me onto the exit for I-55 South.

Within minutes I crossed the line into Mississippi.

You get to a point where you no longer measure in miles or minutes. The highway rolls by, this stretch and that stretch become the same, and sometimes a couple hundred miles and minutes vanish. You're someplace else. And you feel all right that you don't know where you are because something inside you says that you're headed somewhere and that somewhere is where you're supposed to be. I was on that path. Maybe Chloe was. Maybe Pete was.

In Jackson, I stopped for gas. I pulled out my credit card and for the second time Chloe's picture came out with it. The clerk, a handsome young guy with rust colored hair, handed the photo back to me without looking at it. His name tag said Robert Kearns. He was waiting for the charge to clear. "Keep it, Robert," I said. He looked up at me, then down again at the picture.

"Oh," he said. "She's a pretty thing, ain't she?" He slid the picture toward me.

"Keep it," I said again. "She's a movie star." He was studying the picture now.

"What's her name?"

"Chloe."

"Chloe what?"

"Chloe Star."

There was a storm blowing in from the gulf. The sky was blue, but way south the darker clouds piled up, one stack over another. For about the fiftieth time, my boys were reminding me that Tuesday's gone, and I'm in that no-place, no-time zone when I see the exit for McComb. I'm searching, but I still don't know what for.

McComb could be any place. Could be Darlington, where I started. Where I used to live. Where I once worked as a plumber for Pete Hump, my once best friend. Where I once had a wife.

The sky looked bruised. I felt the temperature falling. Outside Sam Beckett's Bait and Tackle, I parked and entered the black clapboard shop. For a second the words "bait" and "tackle" did a rollercoaster ride inside my head. Bait, fish, jail bait, bait and switch, tackle, linebacker, touchdown, Coach, history.

The thinking part had shut down. I asked Sam Beckett, a man of about sixty with an angular face and a bourbon-battered arrowhead nose, for directions. Words covered with Louisiana sauce, words I knew, dripped from his mouth. But I couldn't follow a thing he was saying. Finally, he took me by the arm and led me to the window. He pointed. "Turn there," he said. "About nine miles. Keep yo' eyes open, there's a homemade marker."

I hadn't gone nine miles, and I didn't see anything like a swamp, but I saw a marker, so I pulled over. The sign said, Birthplace of Bo Diddley, December 30th, 1928. But then it also said his name was Ellas Bates. I drove off wondering who really had been born there.

The narrow country two-lane coursed through waist high waves of rich, green cotton. Dark shadows splotched the blacktop that softly turned and sloped down to lowland and water. Ahead, the wind blew hard and the oaks and pines trembled and swayed, Spanish moss trailing behind like white banners. I shut off the music and lowered my window to the cool, damp air. The sky looked like night, felt like night coming. Way off I heard deep, jarring thunder. A swamp smell suddenly filled the cab the way freshly turned soil or the scent of the ocean does.

Looking over to my right, I saw its broad white wings suddenly ascend like a paperwhite petal in the stiff breeze, luminous against the black storm clouds, so bright that light seemed to come from inside the crane. I held my breath. I felt it coming. And around the next curve I saw the marker, a slab of white marble in the shape of a bird.

Just as I parked, the first raindrops came down like quarters on the windshield. The thunder was closer. I shut my eyes and listened to the rain for a few seconds. A flash of lightning lit up behind my closed lids.

I stepped outside into the storm. In only moments my skin was soaked. Falling back against the truck, I studied the marble slab as giant drops of water dripped from my nose and cheeks. October 20, 1977, it said. The rain came down harder. I shielded my eyes then lifted them to the angry sky. A murky line of black clouds pulled away from the others and trailed down like sheer, black dancing dresses then dipped below the swirling, blissful trees. Looking out above the swampy woods, I conjured the Convair, its line of descent, and awaited without blinking its fatal fall.

I wanted to comfort and console them, to say they weren't all alone in their final moments. I narrowed my eyes against the rain and tried with all I had to create the picture of that plane coming down.

72

But I couldn't do it.

Instead, the smell of the swamp became the smell of Lake Mattamuskett and the thunder and the rain were of that lake. I am alongside the bass boat gathering our rods and reels, trying to beat the storm while Pete backs the trailer toward the landing. I see young Pete squinting through the back glass, his arm hugging the seat, his mouth doing that funny twisted up thing as he steers in little jerking motions, aiming the trailer back toward me.

Then a *zing*.

Not a piercing sound, and not the wind, though I am surrounded and held up by a mighty wind. My eyes are closed but I am seeing. Pictures flash before me. I can't say it's my life, these vivid moments from my past. I witness events and people I've forgotten now, things I wish I could remember. But the light I remember. The light I'll never forget. I can't describe it as light—as "vibration" doesn't describe music. Imagine light as smell. Crack open an ice cold ripe watermelon. That burst of air from the heart of the melon, were it light, that would be it.

I'm surrounded by that thing that is and isn't light when all at once I see freshly turned fertile black earth, a vast, empty field. A ragged carnival tent stands before me. Hot summer sunlight illuminates the canvas and its warm sweet aroma fills the air. From inside the tent a choir sings. The broad canvas flaps part and I float inside. There before me on the candlelit stage, naked brown peasant women, heavy-breasted and thick-thighed, slowly swoon as they wail *When Love Finds You*. I'm drawn to them and all my burdens are lifted.

Then I'm suddenly way up looking down at Pete and me, Pete crying, pounding my chest. Next, I'm lying on my back in his arms. A funny singed smell surrounds everything. Raindrops pelt my face.

I open my eyes. "Watch 'em dance," I say.

"In a giant tent. In an open field," Pete says.

Thick steam rises from the blacktop and drifts around me. I reach inside the steel toolbox behind the cab of Pete Hump's #2 for my boat cushion. There is bourbon under the seat. I'm sopping wet. Cool gray sheets of rain wash over me. I drop the cushion beside the Free Bird marble slab, prepare to sit and drink and think. Then I decide I ought to stand while I drink.

My steady eyes watch the dark tide of clouds and the blinding flashes of light. The earth trembles. But I'm not cold. I'm not hungry. I'll wait it out. The rain feels good on my bruised and cut hands. I tilt up the bottle and water trails down my face. I look up again. I'm at that place between holding on and moving on. Looking. Waiting.

Eyes open.

And if there's a bolt of lightning forming up there, searching for its bright, destined path across the sky, awaiting its mark, I'll see it coming. I will.

Chloe

If this were a movie, you'd witness its opening scene from way up here. Think God's eye view.

It is dawn. Artificial fog. Sort of a fifties noir effect. Far below, through a break in the haze, a knockout blonde wearing a low-cut red and white poka dot swings a ten pound sledge, pummeling the front bumper of a green pickup. Very deliberately. Taking her time.

You're too far up to hear the wallops. But even from this distance you're already hoping she'll appear naked in your movie. Her name is Chloe, and she's everything you ever dreamed of having or being. And you're wondering why she's doing a number on the green truck parked in the middle of an isolated lot in what you'll soon learn is an old section of Memphis.

You're hoping now for a close-up. Because when the glamour girl in the polka dots takes that hammer back, the result is poetic harmony in form and movement, something iconic about that snapshot instant, arms extended to the heavens, head tossed back, a kind of vintage pin-up pose. Her perfect figure becomes an indelible freeze-frame locked inside your imagination. But exceeding your visceral, erotic response is curiosity: who *is* this polka dot avenger and why is she assaulting the green truck's bumper?

Cut to the eyes of the male lead, Pete Hump, who slowly wakes to a terrifying realization. His head and hands are duct taped to the steering wheel. Waking is a painful thing and Pete, who looks a lot like Nicholas Cage, is still drunk from the night before. His startled eyes search for help, find none. He passes out again, and we enter Pete's dream, a flashback:

Pete and Chloe in bed inside their sinful love nest in Charleston, South Carolina. In the dream, he wakes at Chloe's touch. Soon the two are entwined in a kind of horizontal slow dance. She coos in a hot, bourbon scented voice: "Pete Hump's Heat Pumps," and they go at it. This in part satisfies our longing to see Chloe's delicious flesh while

75

giving us a context for the opening scene.

Then we're back with wide-eyed Pete, who doesn't so much hear Chloe's heavy hammer probing his bumper as he feels the hammer's vibration, like a ball-peen on an anvil. Each stroke lands in perfect time to Lynard Skynard's *Free Bird*.

Next, in a flashback we get back story on Pete Hump.

Extreme close-up: Pete's bloody face looks like somebody dunked his head into a blender. In fact it takes us a second to realize it *is* Pete Hump. The camera slowly pulls back to reveal:

Night in a wide, empty lot. Pete teeters on his knees, his hands taped behind him. Hanging far away in the black sky is a lighted billboard for his plumbing company. Looming in the darkness, a giant of a man towers over the kneeling Pete Hump. Shot from a low angle, the enormous man appears to have a block head, meant to suggest Frankenstein and thus evoke fear and pity in us. We will learn that he is Chloe's husband, Russ Watts.

"This is the last time I'm asking, Pete," Russ says. "Where is she?" Russ has clobbered Pete into a near-death experience. And now we know why.

The hands of Russ, the cuckold, attach one end of heavy copper jumper cables to the battery terminals of Pete Hump's Truck #2. We wince and want to look away when he slowly clamps the other end of one cable to Pete's right ear. Pete squenches shut his eyes. When the teeth of the second cable shut down on his other ear, we see the trickle of blood there and wait in perverse and collective wonder for some high-tech special effect and the thrill of the sudden fiery eruption from the top of Pete's head. His pleading eyes bend up to us.

Wrapped around Russ' fist is a wire lead that trails to the throttle arm of the truck's engine. Russ pulls the lead and the motor howls, Wa-WOWWWWWW. The green pickup's headlights quiver. Pete's eyes look like a Betty Davis Chihuahua's eyes. But at that moment of intense macabre anticipation, this flashback abruptly ends.

We return to the knockout in the red and white polka dot dress somewhere in Memphis.

"Chloeee?" Pete shouts in that pleading, whiny Nicholas Cage voice, "What are you doin', darlin'?"

Chloe pauses from her Barry Bonds number and wipes a blonde ringlet from her damp cheek.

"I'm searching, Pete."

"What for, darlin'?" Pete calls.

"The connection," she answers.

"Me, too, Chloe. Me, too, darlin'."

"No," she says. "There is a sensor somewhere on this bumper, and when I strike it just right, your brains will go flying against the back glass of Pete Hump's Truck #1."

Cult fans of the film *Pulp Fiction* about wet their pants.

Pete, who looks a lot like Cage in *Raising Arizona*, pleads, "Chloe!" He draws a deep, hopeful breath. The hammering resumes. We really want another look at Chloe, but we don't get it. This, we know, is a tease.

"Chloeeee!"

Fighting now to free his duct-taped hands, Pete squirms from side to side. He looks like he's dancing The Charleston. Again the hammering stops. Pete opens his eyes and slowly rolls them way, way up.

Chloe stands at the driver's side window. She's worked up a sweat, and her blonde hair falls in thin wiggly crescents over her cheeks. Her face is moist and flush. Male or female, you feel a stirring down there. And so even under dire circumstances, Pete's whanger does a summersault. She is the most beautiful woman you and Pete and I have ever seen. Her perfect lips move, but he can't read them. He doesn't want to read them. He just wants to watch them move. She tilts her head to the side then steps out of the frame.

Pete waits for the pounding to resume, knowing, as we do, that with every blow the law of averages turns a little more against him, that when Chloe finally strikes the hidden sensor he will see the big light that Russ Watts saw when he was struck by lightning, only Pete won't come back from that eternal tunnel. We wiggle in anticipation of the Quentin Tarantino reverse-angle splatter moment. We can't wait.

Through the magic of surround-sound and a gazillion speakers, we hear the echo of Pete's hyperventilating inside his head.

A bright light nearly blinds us.

In that suspended moment, subliminal edits remind us of the jumper cables attached to Pete's ears, the taut wire tugging the throttle arm, and we again experience the titillating anticipation of Pete's blown head gasket.

Pete's eyes fly open.

The dazzling morning sun at her back, Chloe stands before the pickup's open door in breathtaking, hourglass silhouette—holding a dagger, a six-inch metal fingernail file. Tears puddle her eyes. (The ghastly look of Pete's reaction in this shot will become the focal point of the poster outside the theater entrance.) Her dagger-loaded fist goes up and up, Hitchcock-like, and every hair at the base of our collective neck stands at attention.

Chloe's fingers cover his eyes.

"Chloe, please," he whimpers in that hangdog Nick Cage voice.

What follows is a digitized, slow motion blur: David Lynch-like, the sharp tip of the nail file *explodes* through the duct tape and enters Pete's ear canal.

Her fingers ease away from Pete's wide, wild eyes. No pain there. His hearing returns, as if he has surfaced from deep water. The white noise he'd heard is Lynard Skynard singing *Free Bird* on the two-way radio.

"Last chance, Pete," Chloe says. "Say you'll let me go."

If he could say it, he would. She just looks at him.

"Bye," she says.

Then she slams the door to Pete Hump's #1 and walks out of his life.

All of this happens in maybe three minutes. The hope is that you'll remain completely under the story's spell for seven more minutes. If you're not immersed by the ten minute mark, it's a good bet this movie will lose money.

Chloe walks, and we are with her. In the distance, Pete's pleading voice echoes from inside the truck cab. The Van Zant boys wail in the background. Chloe doesn't look back. We track along beside her, the pain on her face telling us that her heart falls a notch each time he calls her name, like it fell when her husband Russ pleaded for her to stay. The way it has when every man who ever called her his watched her walk away. Still, she takes a deep, determined breath and lifts that gorgeous, suffering face to the Memphis morning sun. She's not turning back. Because now it is *her* heart she's trying to save.

Somewhere, somehow, there is something better waiting for her, a stronger, truer voice calling—a voice that has been speaking to her all her life. A voice she has resisted until now.

The voice of Don LaFontaine, the movie trailer guy.

Before the show is over, we'll learn how that voice summoned her to Dollywood and cried out to her at Graceland. But for now, all we know is that there is no turning back.

Behind her, a brilliant orange sunrise fills the screen, and we oooh and ahhh at the heavy symbolism. Chloe grips her purse and at a snappy Dolly Parton pace puts as much distance as she can between herself and Pete's sad begging.

There's more in that walk than any acting school can teach.

"Once you know a thing," she says to us, "you can't *not* know it. It's better to be a one hit wonder than to spend your whole life wondering." And we all nod a big uh-huh.

In this movie, as in all movies, when the cab driver's eyes linger too long in the mirror, we get queasy, especially in Memphis rush hour traffic. Add to our anxiety a maniacal driver in a truck identical to Pete's who, unbeknownst to the cabbie, swerves across lanes like a meth freak, a predator, and our sphincter contracts. To our relief, the fool doing ninety flies past, Skynyrd blasting from the cab of the green truck. Finally the taxi driver says into his mirror, "Ma'am, if I'm wrong, I hope you'll forgive me, but are you a movie actress?"

"No, sir, I'm not," Chloe says in a flat Dolly Parton voice, her eyes never leaving the landscape that once belonged to Elvis.

"Are you in the stories? On TV?"

Chloe gently turns her head from side to side.

After the cab driver drops her off at the car rental place, his mouth opens involuntarily, and he whispers reverently: "Them's the finest fashion accessories I ever laid eyes on." The driver is a quiet man and a good Christian by Memphis standards, and he considers himself a professional. He respects people's privacy as he respects his own. But this woman makes him violate standard taxi driver protocol.

"The very finest," the driver laments as she walks away. He can't stop himself from looking into his mirror one last time as she disappears into the rental office.

At this point, about the five-minute mark, we suspect that what we have here is a quest story, that Chloe is in search of something essential to her being, that from now on we're in for a journey of self-discovery, a chick flick.

Cut to Chloe at the wheel of her rental, something classic like a Mustang. She drives slowly across the lot and in a close-up interior shot inhales deeply the new car smell. When she stops at the street, she doesn't know which way to turn. Literally. She turns right...gets this look on her face...then jerks the wheel. Horns blow, black smoke everywhere. There must be sixty edits. The spin makes us dizzy.

Chloe completes the U-turn, looks up into our eyes and says, "I've spent my whole life going with the flow." In answer to that realization, we see her foot stomp the gas pedal. A cloud of burning rubber spews from the asphalt. And because that's exactly what we've spent *our* life doing and because she is everything we ever dreamed of having or being, we do a silent little hell yeah and reach for the popcorn.

She drives I-40 with her window down, hair flying in the breeze, the radio softly playing. We hear the intro to what will become Chloe's theme, a Dolly Parton song made famous by Whitney Houston. Although we don't think about it at the time because of her stunning, mysterious beauty, the editor works in shots of her crossing various bridges before we see a road sign telling us that Chloe's destination is Nashville.

When a Skynyrd song, *Searching*, comes on the radio, Chloe quickly shuts it off. Still, the song serves as soundtrack for the following series of flashbacks:

She and a bruised Pete standing at the gates of Graceland, Chloe with her forbidding hand against his chest. "I have to do this thing alone," she says. The look on Pete's face tells us he's already lost her.

When she returns to those gates at closing time, crestfallen Pete-slash-Nick Cage is still waiting, but we know that he's a desperate, broken man.

Later at The Blue Suede Shoes Bar, the camera slowly circles the two of them. We can't hear what Chloe is saying, but we see that she's pouring out her heart to Pete, that saying these things is painful for her, but she is in a struggle for her being. "Sometimes," she says in a sobbing voice, "love and freedom go to war with one another." Pete lifts his bourbon and looks away. "My insides," she says reaching for his hand, "they're filled with those scars."

Pete orders yet another round of drinks and feeds a twenty into the jukebox. Chloe struggles to explain, to spare Pete Hump's heart, while *Free Bird* and *You've Lost That Loving Feeling* play back-to-back until the bartender unplugs the machine. Finally, Pete pushes his glass away and says, "Whatever makes you happy, Chloe." And she hopes against hope, as do we, that it has been settled.

They're inside Pete Hump's #1. Pete fingers the truck key, pauses and looks down at the steering wheel—which we now realize holds the power to blow away his brains—and says, "I can't let you go." Then he starts the engine and pulls out of The Blue Suede Shoes lot. Chloe tries to hold back her anger and her tears, but the bourbon has thinned her skin and exposed her heart. When Pete parks outside the abandoned trucking company in the heart of old Memphis, it's all Chloe can do to hold her emotions in check.

Recognizing that the inevitable end of their love is near, Pete reaches back for all that he has left. He switches off the engine and fishes the bourbon bottle from under his seat. "We're sitting right here," he says in that sweating and crying Nick Cage voice, "until we get this worked out."

We experience the sensation of bombs going off inside Chloe, for Pete's love is true and his devotion written in the cuts and bruises on his face. In a final act of desperation, he plays his last card: "After all I've been through for you—," he says. We don't blame him. We'd say it too. But we're at the ten-minute mark, and we know that Pete might as well be holding Chloe's head under water. And we can't stand that. So when Pete says he can never let her go, dangles his truck key over his open mouth like a goldfish and then washes the key down with bourbon, we gasp for Chloe, who reaches for the bottle and brings it down like a hammer on Pete Hump's drunken head. When she lifts the roll of duct tape like a trophy, we applaud.

If this were a movie, we would be at the end of part one. But this isn't a movie. This is real.

If it were a chick flick, we might cut to an establishing shot or two of Nashville, then to Chloe standing outside the Grand Ole Opry in the black night. She finds her way inside, then up onto the dark stage, and there she bares her soul in a rendition of *I Will Always Love You*, her way of saying goodbye to her past, to Pete and Russ. We see her tears and choke back our own. And we're not the only ones. The ancient custodian who has swept those sacred floors since the days of Hank Williams, Sr. watches too. A key light traces the path of a single tear down his ruddy cheek.

The security guards who take Chloe away are more the hard-hearted type.

The thread that holds this plot together is Chloe's attempt to break into country music. If this were a movie, which it is not, she'd have the talent but can't get the breaks, which is the way we all feel about ourselves.

From now until the end of the third act, things would go from bad to worse for Chloe, and if the movie is to be a success, those things will have to be even worse than we can imagine. She will find and lose the love of her life, a man very much like Clint Black. And if that isn't enough, she'll have a miscarriage after their love falls apart. If that still doesn't do it, the young misguided fan who makes Chloe her hero and upon whom Chloe turns her back because she simply can't carry another ounce of emotional baggage will get run down by a bus owned by a Country music star. At the end of the third act, after it becomes known throughout Nashville that Chloe is responsible for the girl-in-the-coma who adores her, and that the bus accident is likely to ruin the career of someone who holds a striking resemblance to Clint Black, we know that she'll never get work in this town.

But deep down something tells us that we're closing in on Act IV, and though we can't figure out how the hell she's gonna bring it off, we know that this is a chick flick after all and that it's bound to end well. We'll leave the theater crying happy tears and boohooing to folks waiting in line for the nine o'clock that they'll love it.

And of course we won't be disappointed.

Because there is that old custodian who drank with Hank and had a thing for Minnie Pearl, and who happens to be like a father to—you guessed it—Dolly Parton.

Or if the producers don't think the Country music-NASCAR audience will buy tickets, they will have the script revised. Before it's over, the screenplay may be rewritten a dozen times. When all is said and done, perhaps the Chloe character becomes a martial arts diva or a Dalmatian. As for now, Chloe, the knockout in the red and white polka dots, still goes to Nashville, but when she stands outside The Grand Ole Opry awaiting a sign from God she gets none.

In the next scene, she finds herself wandering about the Nashville airport then staring up at the lighted destinations, lost and alone. Maybe she spends the night, or even a couple of days there, until someone who may be on a mission from God, some guy in a turtleneck, says to her: "You belong in Hollywood."

In that case, Act III retains much of what was written in the original script, except Chloe is a gifted, struggling actress who repeats most of the mistakes she made as a struggling singer. Finally, at the point when she's devastated by guilt because of the young girl-in-a-coma who idolized her, Chloe is offered a spot in a television commercial in which she is obviously cast as look-alike of her idol, Dolly Parton. The commercial is a smash hit. It's everywhere.

Chloe's big break comes when she's invited to appear on a late-night show that we all know is supposed to be David Letterman. But things go badly. Dave wants to poke fun at and mock Dolly, and Chloe loses her shit—not Dolly's but her own. Brought to tears by the rich and arrogant host, she calls the Letterman impersonator a pencil dick, dumps coffee on his Armani suit, and storms off stage in a display that makes copulating couples all over America stop and stare slack jawed at the screen.

Chloe goes lower, then even lower, then gutter low. When it appears that her only option is returning to either Russ Watts or Pete Hump, both of whom still love her, she thinks seriously of putting out the Big Light when—you guessed it, again—Dolly appears.

That is how cheap fiction works.

But this is not a movie. This is real. And in truth disappointment is for most of us our appointed destiny.

And so Chloe drives to Nashville. Even makes her way to the Grand Ole Opry where she stands outside thinking about Dolly and Elvis, about need and desire, about love and emptiness. But standing there also reminds her of who she really is, a woman who's spent most of her life feeling that she is living in a movie. But life, she knows, is not a movie. She's like us, with this exception: she is cursed with freak beauty and some small degree of talent, just enough to feel the need that drives every artist.

Still *our* need is to think of Chloe as a sexy, liberated woman, a chick-flick starlet who exercises the full range of contemporary feminine prerogative—from innocent victim to atomic estrogen. We want that for ourselves. We're not thinking of Chloe, a breathing agonizing human being who will suffer more for her beauty by watching it fade. There's no way we bought a ticket to spend two hours with a woman blessed with physical perfection and cursed with a single drop of talent—only to have it thrown in our face that no drop at all could have meant a happier life. To learn that she is no more in charge of her life than we of ours? That our heroine discovers she will amount to nothing? No way. Still, there is no negotiating with fate.

This is the cost of serious fiction.

And so this is what we get: At a Nashville truck stop, Chloe pumps her own gas, then heads east on I-40. Like most of us, she is not running to. She's running from. And like us, she doesn't know when to hold on and when to move on. What she says aloud is, "If you can't learn to live with who you are, how, dear God, can you learn to live with who you ain't?" Which we *really* don't want to think about.

Returning from Nashville, she sees a sign for the Great Smoky Mountains. Chloe reflects upon Graceland, Dollywood, Pete Hump and Russ Watts, and what she feels is immeasurable regret and debilitating worthlessness. Now the voice inside says, "You don't want it because you don't need it because you can't have it because you don't deserve it because you don't want it." And on and on.

As the horizon flattens, Chloe stares at the interstate ahead and enters an exhausted trance, a period of mindless absence when a few hours and several hundred miles fold into a place that is no place and a time that is no time. It's not peace that she feels, only the cold comfort of nothingness.

It might be politically correct and convenient to think of Chloe as a victim of advertising and commerce or in terms of a history that has been unkind to women. But that is merely an academic diversion, a sort of intellectual bait-and-switch. We're talking about the human heart here, not a cliché. All Chloe knows is that she can't go back and that the big green sign she just passed says she's two hundred miles from Wilmington, North Carolina and the end of the road—the Atlantic Ocean.

Standing at a gas pump Chloe sees a young girl with Down syndrome. A violent wave of disgust crashes down on her. "For having spent one minute of my life feeling sorry for myself," she whispers. And the cycle of self-loathing begins again. She just wants this darkness to stop, for it to go away, to get outside of her own head. But she can't.

To stop the voice inside she begins reading road signs aloud and discovers that the right combination of sound and image soothes her spirit. "Chapel Hill," she says. She pictures the two, the church upon the hill. Then she says it again, like music, allowing the connotations of "chapel" and the soft vowels and breathy consonants to do their work. Up ahead she sees another sign. "Cary," she whispers, and thinks of her burdens, her obligation to carry on. And later, when she voices, "Fuquay-Varina, Fuquay-Varina, Fuquay-Varina," she is reminded of "sugarplum fairy," and a little smile appears on her lips.

She nears the intersection of I-40, which connects Barstow to Wilmington, and I-95, which runs from New Brunswick to Miami. She can't go forward and she can't turn back. I-95 south would take her to Darlington, South Carolina, where she started, where she's lived her life, where she married a man she never loved and had an affair with his boss, his childhood friend.

Ahead, the interstate sign says Rocky Mount. In spite of the sign's implications, she takes the northbound exit.

Soon she sees a sign for Smithfield, which will inevitably have a Main Street, and on that street live the Smiths, the most common of the common. She is one of them.

Chloe looks up. She has never seen the arrestingly beautiful woman on the billboard. The words under the picture say The Ava Gardner Museum, Smithfield.

The museum hostess touches the nametag above her breast. "I know it looks like 'Deidre'," she says with a pleasant smile, "but I pronounce it 'Dead-ra'." She invites Chloe into a small theater, as quiet and softly lit as a funeral parlor. Chloe enters. A large painting, the poster model for the film *The Barefoot Contessa*, takes Chloe's breath: Ava stands at the edge of a great precipice, her arm extended, one slipper dangles from her fingers. Behind her a man, his face buried in her shoulder, his arms around her, clings in a kind of death grip.

The actress's life is reduced to twelve minutes of video. The woman on the screen, the fetching sex queen on the billboard, was not the real Ava Gardner, the barefoot country girl from Grabtown. She is so stunningly beautiful that Chloe hardly hears the narrator's voice until he says, "She was always searching for the love that was always out of reach."

The hostess lowers her newspaper and smiles.

"Where is she now?" Chloe asks.

As Deidra reaches for a small brochure, Chloe recognizes the woman's look. It asks, Are *you* a movie actress? Are *you* in the stories?

"How long have you been an Ava fan?" she says in her lyrical eastern North Carolina accent, sounding a little like Ava, a little like Chloe.

"All my life," Chloe says. "All my life."

A summer storm is waiting when Chloe steps out of the museum. She can smell it. It reminds her of home.

She parks outside a liquor store.

Sunset Memorial Park is located on Highway 70 in Smithfield. There are strip malls close by, a damaged furniture warehouse outlet and tobacco fields within view.

She parks near the cemetery gate, stuffs the two pints of bourbon into her purse. Slate colored clouds as wide as glaciers gather overhead and the distant drone of thunder whispers far away. She removes her shoes before stepping from the car then surveys the tombstone landscape. A cool, cool breeze lifts the hem of her thin red and white polka dot dress.

Chloe believes that the living can communicate with the dead, and she feels in no hurry to rush out to whatever awaits her. She and Ava will remember walking barefoot along the soft furrows. She'll pour drinks. They will talk of true love and about how to go on living without it. Then she will wait and she will listen. And if the rain comes, she will wait and she will listen.

But standing now at the gates of Sunset Memorial she must commence to begin, as the old people used to say. She must take a first step. There are no identifying markers, no clear directions, no promises. Still, she knows Ava is out there, waiting. It is the one thing Chloe knows, the one certainty, the one sure thing. She will look and listen. Await a sign.

The heavy summer clouds behind her are a dark bruised Technicolor. The cool breeze lifts her blond hair and sculpts the thin dress to her ripe body. Chloe enters the land of the dead.

"Ava?" she whispers. She stops. She listens. "Ava, it's me."

Molly and Joe

Driving home, Molly zigzagged past remnants of her day then purged lists of things to do and buy, unaware of the traffic, the familiar turns, humming the melody as Vince Gill sang softly from the car's speakers. At the stoplight, she turned onto Hampton Street and lifted her hand to shield the afternoon sun. From the wavering tentacles above the long blistering stretch of asphalt, a distant human form, small and transitory, materialized. The quivering specter grew larger, sharper. It was Coach.

"Don't look," she whispered. But she did. And in that snapshot moment, the man's heart exploded and his body seemed to evaporate as his clothes dropped into a heap—that quickly, that unconditionally, down to the ground.

When her husband walked in from work he heard the rising inflection of Molly's voice. "What?" Joe said. "What did you say?"

She sat alone in the pale kitchen light, near the window. "I wasn't talking," she said.

"Okay," he said. He stood in the doorway holding up the day's mail.

"Could we have a beer?" she said.

Joe tilted his head. "Well, *hello*," he said. He held the pose. "You bet. And it's not *even* Sunday night."

"Well, you know," she said, finding her footing. "Harrison—."

Sunday nights, after putting their young son to bed, Molly and Joe drank a beer or two. Sunday night was their designated together time. But Harrison was away now on a fishing trip with his grandfather.

"Two cold ones," Joe said into the refrigerator.

She looked away. "Something happened," Molly began.

"What?" He turned. Gently, deliberately, he set a carton of milk on the counter. "What happened?" He pushed his chair close. "Harrison?"

87

"No," she said.

She described pulling over and rushing to Coach, recounted her fear that he might already be dead. The EMS. The sirens and the rush to the hospital. She thought but did not say: I took his head into my arms. She didn't say: There was more intimacy in that minute than in every minute I've ever spent with you.

"Can we have another?" she said, lifting her empty glass.

"Sure," he whispered, rising slowly from the table.

The two drank, and after a time she described again what she had witnessed, repeating it nearly word for word while the yellow evening light sank into blackness, slowly then all at once, like an exhausted swimmer's drowning. She couldn't stop telling it. Every sentence ended like a question. Then again she came to the end.

Their son was gone. The house was silent.

"No more beer," Joe announced. He turned to his wife. Neither spoke. Her eyes conveyed nothing.

"I'll take you out," he said. "We should get out more," he said, "just the two of us." Joe touched her hair. "Let's have one more. Let's do go," he said. "Then we'll come home. We'll call Harrison."

The lot outside The Paradise Lounge was nearly empty. The only regular sitting at the bar was Vincent Howle, who was sleeping or praying. In the shadows at the far end sat a stranger, a face Joe didn't recognize. Dave and Nick Granger sat at the near end. Their expectant eyes turned to Molly and Joe. They had been Coach's backfield that championship season.

Joe ordered beers. Tami, a part-time waitress, was tending. She wore her signature Hooter's T-shirt turned inside out, but below the short blond hair her face was dark and somber. George Miles, the bartender, and the other regulars would be at the hospital.

"Any word?" Joe asked.

"No," Nick said looking down into his glass.

Joe gave his shoulder a touch, lifted the beers from Tami, and stepped quietly toward his wife. In the first booth beside the door, Molly waited with her back to him. He set a beer in front of her. "Your dad wouldn't let Harrison on a boat without a life preserver, would he?" she said, holding the beer at her lips. "He didn't pack his life jacket. It's hanging in the garage."

"No," her husband said.

"I'm not so sure," she said. "I'm not so sure." Then Molly said,

"Give me your hand."

He pushed his beer over to her side and stood. "No," she said, "just your hand."

The bar was dimly lit, the hum from the red and blue neon beer signs hanging above them the only sound. Molly ordered another round. They drank. When he could no longer bear the compression of their silence, Joe said, "When we finish these, we should go." They both drank. "This is no good," Joe said.

"You're right," she said.

"Okay," Joe said.

"Tell me a secret," she said.

"About what?" he said. "What do you mean?"

"Wanna take turns?" She offed a woozy smile. "A secret. You know. You show me yours," she said, "I'll show you mine?" Lifting her chin, she closed her eyes and leaned in as if to whisper. She fingered the top button of her blouse, released it.

"We should go," he said.

"Yes?" she said in a fetching voice.

"We should go home now," he said.

"Yummy," she said. "Come on. Don't you wanna know a secret?"

He reached for the hand at her blouse, held it. She pulled away, lifted then set down her empty bottle, pressed her palms on the tabletop and slowly stood. "When I get back," she whispered, "my panties will be in my purse."

"I'll pay," he said.

"Good boy," she said. His wife seemed to glide away, toward the restroom. "Just kidding," she called. Then she was not there.

At the other end of the bar, the Granger brothers sat blank-eyed, mute. Joe dug for his wallet and looked up for Tami. She sometimes filled in now for B.B., Coach's wife. B.B. was gone, nobody knew where. At the far end of the bar beyond Vincent Howle and the faceless stranger, Tami stood in a shadow, her back to everything, talking into the phone.

Joe called to her. "I want to settle up."

When she turned, Joe saw the tears on Tami's cheeks.

Vincent Howle glanced up from his prayer. "Are you sure about that?" Vincent's eyes descended in meditation, but he lifted his face as if he'd heard a whisper. "Want to settle up, huh? You better know what the bill is before you say *that*." He turned and called to the crying woman.

"We all got to settle up sometime, right Tami?" She didn't look. "But you don't have to *want* to," he said to Joe. "*I* sure as hell don't want to."

Tami bit her bottom lip and held up one finger.

From the other end of the bar, Nick, who too had seen the tears, called to her. "*Coach*?" he said.

"No," she said to Nick. Choking it back, she pressed the phone tight against her ear, turned away and walked as far as she could walk into the shadows, to the wall, where she buried her eyes into the crook of her arm.

Vincent turned again to Joe. "Are you driving to the hospital?" he said, his eyes glazed with liquor and blood. His sweat smelled of sour bourbon. "I've lost my license," he said.

"No," Joe said. "Must take my wife home now."

"Not really lost. Taken," Vincent said. "Lost is worse." His voice was steady, melodious and clear. "Death is a terrible thing. The only thing worse is lost. I've got to get to the hospital."

Tami set two beers on the bar. Joe turned. "No," he said to her, pushing back the beers. She looked away, down into the phone. The tears had stopped, but her face was still crying.

"Yes. Lost is worse," Vincent said. "Coach, he's treading now."

Without breaking stride, Molly lifted one of the beers and drifted at an angle toward their booth. Joe reached for his own beer. Vincent clasped his arm and looked into his eyes. "Distance from God is loneliness."

Joe couldn't bear Vincent's eyes. "My wife—," he said softly.

"Look at me," Vincent said. "As God is my witness, loneliness is the Devil."

When Joe neared the booth, Molly brushed the seat beside her, an invitation. Joe slid in close. "Good beer," she said, smiling brightly. "Wanna dance?" He saw that she had been crying in the bathroom. "What a day, huh? Left the life preserver hanging in the garage," she said.

"Let's go," he said.

"Let's drink." She leaned forward and issued a cartoon wink. Looking away, she reached for his hand. Joe lifted his wife's fingers, held them. "We could just sit here all night," she said, her eyes on the door, "and maybe go on and on, like when I was in high school. Like when we could just be silent and read each other's mind? Like when I'd, you know, let you do things."

"I didn't know you then," he said.

She turned and pressed her palm against Joe's face and looked at him. "I want us to be like that," she said.

"We should go," he said taking her hand into his.

She lowered her eyes. "Yes," she said. "Let's."

Vincent Howle stood, turned and walked with balanced grace and ease, trailing his hand along the bar. He looked at Molly. When their eyes met, he gave her a gentle smile and raised his hand. "Goodbye," he said. Vincent stopped and spoke to the Granger brothers, and in a minute the three of them left The Paradise Lounge.

Tami had disappeared. The faceless stranger was gone.

Molly and Joe sat looking out onto the empty bar like two strangers waiting at an elevator. And the only sound in the room was the neon murmur of red and blue beer signs.

"Put on your seatbelt," Joe said, fumbling to work the key into the ignition.

"No," she said. "I don't want to."

"It's dangerous," he said.

"Yes?" She gave him a lascivious smile. "Make me?" she whispered.

He unfastened his own seatbelt, then reached over for hers, pulled it across her and buckled it.

She tossed back her hair. "The man, he touched my breasts?" she announced.

Joe backed slowly from the parking space, his every movement premeditated, deliberate. He knew everything depended on him. He still understood consequences.

They were on Cashua Ferry now. No more streetlights. Open road. Molly closed her eyes. "Do you remember that game we played in high school, Truth or Dare?" she said.

"Not now," he said, glancing up into his mirror, giving all he had to getting them home safely. "Besides it takes three to play."

She glided her hand up his thigh. "Baby makes three?" she purred. "Dare me?" she said.

"It's late," he said.

Joe knew that driving too slowly was as likely to get him arrested as speeding, but he still knew the difference. He was drunk, but he'd not lost his concentration. He knew what he had to do to get home safely.

"Remember how amusing you once thought I was? In high school, I mean," Molly said.

"I didn't know you then," he said.

She closed her eyes again and cupped the back of his neck in her palm. "I want to tell you something amusing."

"Okay," he said. "I'd like that." At that moment his vision doubled.

"I can't remember what I was trying to forget."

His concentration deepened. His eyes remained fixed on the vague dark street that unfolded before him. His vision narrowed. Joe's hand levitated from the steering wheel and floated toward his wife's.

"Okay," he said. "Tell me."

"That was the amusing thing. What I just said. 'I can't remember what I was trying to forget?' That was it." She waited for him to reply, but he didn't. She laid back her head and shut her eyes, like an astronaut awaiting launch. "Where are we?" she said.

Headlights appeared in the distance. Could be the cops. Or some drunk teenager. He settled in, found his bearings, glanced down at the speedometer. Drew a deep breath. They would make it home safely now. He'd locked in.

"It's hanging there, collecting dust," she said. "So-to-speak."

"Don't look," he whispered into the brilliant headlights, watching the asphalt rolling in like a giant ocean swell, his eyes wide and ready now, this stretch of road foreign, as if he had never driven it. He gripped the wheel. The advancing headlights swept over Cashua like a white tide, washing the blacktop away. Joe tilted his head, watching obliquely, waiting stiffly for the other car to pass.

Molly released her seatbelt, rested her head on his shoulder. They were suddenly immersed in light. Joe felt her breath on his neck. She whispered something he didn't hear. And then it was over.

Her head lay upon his shoulder, eyes shut. Shadows from the green panel lights disfigured their faces.

"What?" he said. "I didn't hear you."

"Too late now," she said.

"Harrison?"

"I have a bad feeling."

"Almost home. We'll call."

"No. What I was trying to forget?"

He didn't answer. The drone of the engine and her breathing were the only sounds. She opened her eyes, moved away from him against the door and felt for her seatbelt. It was where it always was, within reach but out of sight.

"But it's still there." she said. "Hanging there."

"We're here," he said.

She looked out into the night. "Yes," she said. "I thought so." He shut off the engine. "That's what I thought all along."

Vincent

Sunday, 6 A.M.

Had you seen his eyes from the civilian side of the cell bars, you'd have sworn the man was watching TV. That same vacant, drop-jawed mentally challenged gaze of wonder. The looker was Vincent Howle staring into nothing, searching for connections between losing his wife, being labeled the Devil and landing in jail.

Vincent blinked slowly, then pressed his palms into his eyes. His synapses were impaired, dulled, like seeing the world through a shower curtain. Inside his head, thoughts that ought to have been tiny lightning flashes of clarity and natural good sense were instead a floating muddle of bewilderment surfing a tide of Jack Daniels. I'm in jail, Vincent Howle thought. Again. Then after a pause he listened for a second opinion. "Dear God," he whispered. "This can't be real."

In a deep cave from somewhere around his fifteenth birthday, he heard the preacher's voice. The tall, lanky reverend moved with the robotic actions of a miniature wooden figure that milks a cow when the wind blows just right. "How do we know what is *real*?" the preacher had shouted rhetorically, thrusting his arms up and down then answering his own question before anybody could reply. "What is our *sixth* sense?" he demanded with the rising inflection of a Final Jeopardy answer. "The *sixth-ah* sense is the grace of *G a w d-ah*," he shouted, stretching the Lord's name in a horizon-to-horizon rainbow. "Forgiveness is the *sixth-ah*!" Then swooning like the worst white dancer you ever saw he sang out in that revival voice, "the Fa-ther-*ah*, the Son-*ah*, the Ho-ly Ghost-*tah*," his words loud and rhyming, like Red-Ro-*va*, Red-Ro-*va* send Vincent right O-*va*. Fifteen-year-old Vincent, caught up in the mesmerizing passion of the moment, spontaneously yodeled from a pew near the back, "It's-the 6-*ah*, 6-*ah*, 6-*ah* that's real-*ah*!!" like a ra-ra-ra football cheer.

That night, after a few cold ones he'd bought from a bootlegger at a joint called Best Stretch, Vincent answered the knock at his trailer door, and when he did, four of the church deacons slapped him silly. "We're gonna beat the Devil outta you, boy," one said.

"I'm sorry," Vincent shouted, throwing up his arms against the whirling hive of flying fists. "I didn't mean it," he kept saying as he ducked and dodged.

"6-6-6! You don't know what sorry is!" said another.

With tears slinging from his cheeks, Vincent shouted, "I love you, Lord. I love you, Lord."

Vincent turned from the cell bars. "I'm in *jail*," he said, as if the repetition might jar him loose from a bad dream. Behind him, one of the inmates, another drunk, attempted what looked like one-armed pushups as he steadied himself and urinated against the wall.

"I think I'll take this situation one sense at a time," Vincent said to nobody in particular. *Smells* like drunk whiz against a jail cell wall. *Sounds* like a demolition derby inside my head. *Feels* like cheap tequila when you pass it through your nose. *Tastes* like the tequila that doesn't quite make it all the way. *Looks* like hard time. He totaled the five. Vincent ruled out any possibility of a number six, redemption. "Adds up to some bad luck," he said.

"Bad luck," he said again. His brain was like a dull knife trying to slice and dice what he knew in order to pare some sense out of what he couldn't understand. He remembered walking into The Paradise Lounge the night before, the whole crowd singing *Every Time I Roll The Dice*, and sort of remembered George Miles, the bartender saying, "Bo, you're drunker than a dog," and offering to drive Vincent home. Otherwise, Vincent didn't know where to begin. He thought, Where do you draw the starting line for bad luck?

Correct, a shadowy figure resembling Alex Trebek said.

Did it start the night before with his first drink at The Paradise Lounge, or with the accompanying thoughts of Arnelle and her former lover, Roy?

Limit your responses to a single question, Trebek instructed.

How do you know when you've somehow crossed the line?

Alex stood mute, expressionless. Did bad luck originate for Vincent with the 666 blunder at revival services or before there even was a Vincent? Did it begin with Arnelle's lips on Roy's lips? Would you place the point of bad luck's origin at the moment Vincent opened the bedroom door on Arnelle and Roy?

More specific, Alex instructed.

When you saw the naked back of your wife bronco-riding a man who bellowed the lyrics to *She'll Be Coming Around the Mountain When She Comes?*

"*BINGO!*" Alex said with a tight-lipped smile.

Vincent slowly tilted back his head and shut his eyes, just as he had the night before at the request of the state trooper. "Buddy," Vincent pleaded to Alex, "where does this road come out?"

"Buddy," Alex answered, "hit don't."

Lunchtime, A Few Months Earlier

Surely the bad luck for Arnelle's lover, Trigger, the torso, Roy the Parts Man, arrived the instant Vincent brought down the heavy brass Dale Earnhardt lamp between the man's eyes. Maybe the bad luck for Arnelle came when Vincent then reached for the can of roach spray beside the bed and emptied its combustible contents upon the unconscious man's genitals. Arnelle leapt from the bed holding her sweaty breasts like water balloons and po-goed around the tiny trailer bedroom screaming like a spider monkey on fire until her perfume and lipstick vibrated off the dressing table and the dense cloud of roach killer slowly obscured the view of her shrinking object of affection.

"Get out!" Arnelle screamed over and over, gesturing with her pointer finger toward the door in a winding-up fashion that made her right breast giggle like Jell-O. "Get the hell out!" she yelled. But Vincent was in no hurry to leave the scene of the crime, for although there was no blood, the purple knot at Trigger's hairline climbed and climbed like the magic birth of a unicorn's horn.

"Look," Vincent exclaimed, patting his mouth in mock surprise, "his forehead is getting a hard-on."

"Get out!" Arnelle said again, "I hate your guts."

"I'll leave when I'm good and ready," Vincent shouted back. Arnelle gave him a vaporizing X-ray glare, huffed and knifed her hands against her hips like an NFL official signaling an emphatic offside.

"Those yours or his?" Vincent said with a nod toward the red fingerprints on her breasts.

"Mine," she snarled, "and you better get a good look now. You better get a eyeful."

Before Vincent could reply, the eyes of the man with the exterminator's smell sprang open so fast they made a sound. His hands flew down to his turtle head penis and his eyes rolled back like a shark's. "*Burn! Ah! Burn! Ah! Burn! Ah!* " he testified, sucking air between his words. Vincent and Arnelle watched as his spit spray settled gentle as

97

dust motes upon his purple horn.

Naked Arnelle huffed a second time. "I'm getting him a wet rag," she declared, charging into the bathroom. She heard Vincent on the porch. "Go back to hell, you *devil*," she shouted, thinking he was out the door. She shut off the spigot with such force she wrung the cheap handle.

"I been there my whole life," Vincent whispered.

At the bathroom door, Arnelle's hand fell open involuntarily, and the wet rag she held dropped from her fingers onto the pink pedicure Trigger had purchased as a lover's gift. She stood motionless and wide-eyed, watching a grin form on Vincent's lips as he set the bloody red metal fire extinguisher on the floor beside the spent can of roach bomb. Trigger's sightless, still eyes had that look of surprise and awe you associate with a child's first fireworks display, and his gaping mouth suggested a moment of revelation frozen at the point of utterance.

A Few Weeks Ago

At the trial, Arnelle wore the square dancing dress Vincent bought her when they took lessons. The tall collar circled her neck like a stovepipe and made pancakes of her breasts. She toted her Bible to the stand with both hands, like an offering.

Arnelle didn't tell the court about the song and dance she'd been up to when Vincent opened the bedroom door, but when she described the clank of the Dale Earnhardt lamp on the victim's head, the dreadful sound and smell of the toxic cloud that hissed from the spray can and hovered above his genitalia, she didn't miss a lick. Under oath, she paid no attention to the laws forbidding any accounts, descriptions or reproductions. For her detailed depiction of the fire extinguisher moment plagiarized the exact diction, cadence, and inflection of the Atlanta Braves announcer's account of an Andruw Jones grand slam.

When the victim was asked to take the stand, Roy leaned upon an aluminum walker and pushed forward as if a mighty wind opposed him. His feet dragged like he was roller skating through mud, which made his hips wobble like a road scraper's tires. Every inch of his painful journey was fake, you could just tell. At the stand, he turned his back to the room and hoisted his privates and grimaced as he eased onto the witness stand.

Roy testified that he and Arnelle met when Vincent sent her to buy hydraulic fluid at the Darlington Auto Supply. "Yeah," Roy said, wrestling back a horse-faced grin, "they call me the *Parts* Man." When

Vincent looked over, he caught Arnelle giving the witness a sly wink.

That Sunday, 10 A.M.

Vincent stood at the cell door rocking from side to side, wondering if that was Arnelle behind the shower curtain. The answer came when she said, "I have a thesis statement for you, Vincent." When they first met Arnelle was enrolled at Florence-Darlington Technical College, where she'd learned about thesis statements and read Bobbie Ann Mason. "I really like Bobbie Ann Mason's thesis statements," she said to Vincent. And ever since, when she had something of gravity to say, she'd start off by saying she had a thesis statement for him.

The cell door opened, the shower curtain parted, and Vincent smiled. "Arnelle," he sang out, "Hallelujah." The words assaulted his tender bourbon-soaked head like a rapping crankhead's Blaupunkts.

"Shut up," Arnelle said.

Sunday, 11 A.M.

He didn't say a word during the processing phase of his release and he didn't intend to engage in any lengthy conversation in the car either. But as Arnelle drove, Vincent saw in her face that she had other plans, that she was biding her time.

He lowered his window. The smell of corn silk and rich, wet freshly turned black soil rushed in. He saw that the tobacco had been topped and suckered, but he didn't like the sound of those words, for his wife had been topped and he suckered. He wiped the beaded sweat from his face and felt the sour liquor seeping out.

"I want to save our marriage," Arnelle said, looking ahead at the unfolding blacktop.

"Okay," Vincent said.

"I made a mistake," she said, like she'd forgotten to carry a one when she did her checkbook arithmetic, as matter-a-fact as saying a dog had ticks.

"What would that be?" he said. "That saving part?" She wouldn't look at him.

"Roy was not what I thought he was."

"What part was different?"

"Now you're trying to pick a fight." She cut her eyes at him, then looked ahead. "If you want to be like that—," she said, letting it trail off. In a minute, she said, "I forgive you, Vincent."

99

Vincent looked out at the black, muddy fields and at the road ahead. Everything was off kilter, everything skewed. When trouble came, all of nature ran for safety, you'd think. But evidence pointed in the other direction. From Mechanicsville to the river, Cashua Ferry Road was littered with road kill: a dead doe, blacksnakes and water moccasins, squirrels, one dead dog and a bushel basketful of squashed possums. The world was on a kamikaze mission, seemed like, everything racing to meet the finish line. He sat here with his wife who was offering to forgive him for cold-cocking her lover in the middle of an equestrian moment. The laws of forgiveness were all out of whack. For Vincent, Mr. 666, there was no setting them right.

"Truth," he said. "Did you quit him just because he failed at cheatin' the insurance company?"

"It wasn't the insurance company, exactly," she said.

"Arnelle, don't get all technical and shit on me now."

"It was a malpractice suit against the emergency room doctor."

"You're getting all technical and shit; I'm asking you why you quit him."

"I'll forgive you, Vincent, under one condition."

"You'll forgive me, huh? You don't know no more about redemption than I do."

"Listen to my thesis statement, Vincent. I'll forgive you if you agree to renew our vows. In church. I figure that's where we went wrong, not getting married in church. On account of what you once done, testifying for the Devil. Our marriage was never sanctified. That's why things didn't work out."

"That ain't what you told me before. You said things didn't work out because Roy couldn't wash the taste of Black Flag off his whanger, that's what you once said."

"He dropped the charges, didn't he?"

"Whose idea was that?"

"He dropped 'em, didn't he?"

"He dropped 'em all right, and the charges ain't all he dropped."

"Don't you dare say that ugly word," she said, "don't you dare."

"You wouldn't happen to have another thesis statement handy there would you, Arnelle?"

Vincent felt the tires leave the asphalt. When he looked over, Arnelle gave the wheel a hard right turn. He threw both hands against the dash. The ditch bank caved. The tires sank fast, and the Honda slowly laid over on its side, like an old fat sow, but with enough momentum for the wet, black earth to peel up through Vincent's window with the action of a snowplow. The car came to a smooth stop. A high, whirling sound filled its interior.

"Damn," Vincent said, shaking his face from side to side. "*Damn*—Arnelle?" He spit once, wiping the mud from his eyes and his raccoon face. Above him, his wife held firmly to the steering wheel, hovering over it with the body English you sometimes observe in NASCAR types atop their riding mowers. "Take your foot *off* the gas," Vincent said. "It ain't doing you no good." The whining sound of the one tire in the mud dropped to a moan. He wiped his face again.

"*Damn*," Vincent repeated. He looked up at Arnelle, who continued gripping and humping the wheel, imploring the Honda to go, go, go. "Shut off the engine, unbuckle your seatbelt and climb out the window," he said. The liquor that remained in his head settled now on the right side of his brain, and the force of gravity made him feel as if he were pinned sideways like an insect in a shadowbox. "Roll down the window and climb on out," he said.

Arnelle reached for the radio. A Neil Diamond song was on the Oldies station. "Promise," she said, staring straight ahead.

"What!"

"You know what. In church, too. I want to hear a thesis statement."

"You just tried to *kill* us, Arnelle. Now roll down your window, undo your seatbelt and climb the hell out," Vincent said.

"Not before you promise. It's the Lord's will," she said.

Vincent's right arm and leg were starting to numb up. "Roll down that window."

"In conclusion," Arnelle said, "I'll repeat my thesis statement: I forgive you, Vincent."

"For all I know, Arnelle, the tailpipe could be choked with mud. We could be inhaling deadly fumes."

"I've been breathing them aplenty," she said, looking away from him.

"I think I'm getting sleepy, Arnelle."

"Till death do us part," she whispered, her voice breaking up in a squeak.

Vincent studied his wife's face. She looked like a little girl with an old woman's face. She looked so sad.

"*He* quit you, didn't he?" Vincent said in a soft voice. "That's what this is all about. He quit *you*."

101

She reached for the radio, turned the volume up real loud.

"You loved him and he didn't love you back," Vincent whispered to himself, looking at his wife, her hair pointing like a cone below her ear, the tears zigzagging off her nose then sliding sideways off her cheek. He felt his heart swell against his chest until it might split in two.

She began singing Neil Diamond at the top of her lungs. A song about reaching out and touching.

Vincent felt something coming up—nothing like bad liquor, something way down there. Coming up sure, resting finally in the center of his chest, opening up to bleed or bloom. With effort, his outstretched fingers, unsteady as a newborn's, floated near her face.

Arnelle tossed her head from side to side and sang loud and out of tune. Vincent slowly rested back as if awaiting liftoff and studied her face with wonder.

"He broke your heart," he said. He crossed his hands and shut his eyes. "I'm so sorry."

"You're sorry?" Arnelle said, sobbing, repeating his words like a song in which the answer is in the question, turning her head from side to side, signaling an unconditional No. "You forgive me?" she kept saying, nodding like it was bad, bad news.

Coach and B.B.

Scaggs Newcomb was a drunk who drove a Mercury and who seemed like a loose-limbed good old Howdy Doody boy but was something else and burned for money. His former cellmate Billy Roberts was a Lincoln Continental man.

On New Year's Eve Billy wrecked the black Lincoln in Charlotte, but the car still drove all right. He and the insurance man didn't see eye-to-eye on the settlement. Billy threw the first punch. Scaggs posted bail.

Squalling the Mercury's tires as he pulled onto East Fourth Street from the Mecklenburg County Jail, that Howdy Doody smile all over his face, Scaggs told Billy he had an idea. They would drive the mangled Lincoln to New Orleans where he said they would chill.

The night before Mardi Gras ended, Scaggs, who had been drinking mescal and snorting cocaine for three days, woke Billy at four in the morning. Billy heard the metal motel door open and shut. The room was black. He could smell Scaggs, but he couldn't see him. The other man was just a smell and a spooky mescal cocaine voice.

"If there's anything in there you want," Scaggs whispered from another world, "you better get the fuck up and come get it." Billy didn't answer. "Stay put," Scaggs said.

Roberts closed his eyes. But not for long. Because of the sirens outside and the smell of burning tires that seeped around the motel windows and beneath the door, wafting sinuously through the stench Scaggs had left in the room.

Later that afternoon, the two men boarded a plane with first-class tickets Scaggs had purchased a month before. They ordered a Maker's Mark before buckling their seatbelts. As the plane lifted off, Scaggs turned to Billy.

"Some people hate that burning smell," he said with his signature grin. He lifted his glass to Billy. "I don't happen to be one of 'em."

That was in February. Billy's trial was set for early August. The plastic surgery had helped some, but the insurance guy's face was still a mess. Stepping out of his lawyer's office Billy saw the Mercury at the curb.

For the July 4th holiday, the two men left Charlotte for Myrtle Beach where Scaggs said they would chill. But when the Mercury reached Darlington, South Carolina, Scaggs didn't take the Highway 52 by-pass. Billy asked why. Scaggs looked up at the city limits sign, then over at Billy and smiled.

Now it was midnight and the two sat in a small NASCAR town, at the bar inside The Paradise Lounge. Except for the kid in the stockroom and the redhead, the place was empty.

"Where's the insurance man?" Billy said.

"At the bank, writing a check," Scaggs said.

"Wrong."

"Banging the wife of the New Orleans Fire Chief?"

"I like it, but wrong again," Billy said.

"At the airport, still scratching his head. Trying to figure out how the *hell* I got us first class tickets out of New Orleans in the middle of Mardi Gras," Scaggs said tossing up a high-five.

"Ding, ding, ding," Billy said, eyeing The Paradise Lounge bartender.

Scaggs signaled again to the redhead. As she reached for two clean glasses and cheap bourbon, Scaggs and Billy watched. Their eyes were all over her. She set the drinks on the bar in front of them. Scaggs spoke to her breasts. "I love them great big—eyes," he said, looking up. "Bright as high beams." He smiled for Billy but his eyes didn't move. "The eyes tell the story." She didn't speak. She turned and walked away. The eyes of men were nothing new to her. "Can't take a compliment?" Scaggs called. "Where I come from, we learn some manners, lady." The two studied her head to foot as they had after every drink.

From the rear storage room where he was sweeping up, Ryan, who was only sixteen, saw the look the men shared. He knew what it meant though he had never been with a woman. The boy's face was potted with acne scars. There was no controlling his thick collie-colored hair. But Ryan's pale blue eyes and gentle, disarming smile brought a kind of invisible friendliness to The Paradise Lounge, and its regulars were united by shared custody of the kid. What most of them had never had or what had been irretrievably lost to them, they could still see in him.

The boy watched B.B.'s face as she walked to the cash register and, beyond her, the faces of the two men who were working her over with their eyes. Then he lifted his broom and began again, glancing back as he swept.

"She's married," Billy said. "Wearing a ring."

"Married is as married does," Scaggs said. "Built like that? Working here? No way."

"How would you know?"

Scaggs closed his eyes and pointed to his temple like a sage. "I know that smell." The door opened and shut. A man, sandy crew cut, faded yellow golf shirt, made for a table beside the jukebox then sat facing the wall.

"I'll be back," Scaggs said. "Stay put. Keep an eye on her."

"With pleasure. You bet. I'd take out some insurance on that if I was her husband," Billy said, smiling, studying the slight sway beneath the thin blouse as she towel-dried highball glasses.

B.B. glanced up into the mirror. Then up again, following Scaggs as he snaked between the tables toward the jukebox. She'd seen out-of-towners shift about then slither away without paying when her back was turned.

Billy looked from B.B. over to Scaggs, lifted his glass and smiled into it.

The man in the yellow golf shirt didn't speak when Scaggs sat across from him. Instead, the man stood, stepped away from the table, and fed a dollar into the jukebox. He punched up George Jones then walked back to his chair.

The man and Scaggs huddled as they talked.

Billy's eyes, drawn by the special way she was put together, settled on B.B. Her body's mechanics were shorthand for fuck me, he thought. He signaled for another drink.

"How's about some breakfast," he said, his eyes ravaging her as she set down a new coaster, then his drink on top, "after you're done here."

"No thanks," she said, wiping the bar where his glass had been.

"A little over-easy?" Billy said leaning in confidentially, his eyes wide and greedy. "Or are you the scrambled, covered, and smothered type?" B.B. didn't look at him, didn't answer.

When she turned, he took her wrist.

"I hear you're not very married," Billy said.

Ryan dropped his broom.

"You need to get your ears checked," B.B. said, prying away his fingers then walking away. She nodded to Ryan. He stopped in his tracks. She nodded a second time and he slowly returned to his work.

"Keep an eye on him," she said. "If he starts anything, call the cops."

"Yes, ma'am." Ryan smiled and rubbed circles on his chest. "Shinin' armor," he said. The boy looked back over B.B.'s shoulder. His smile turned to a scowl. "The other man's gone."

Scaggs and the man in the yellow shirt had left together.

"Shit," she said.

Billy watched as she tossed the bar rag and marched toward him, his eyes following the harmonious sway of her body, the way the parts worked in sync.

"Your friend just walked out on his tab. You picking it up?"

He tilted his head and flashed her a look. "That depends," he said. "On how nice you are to me."

B.B. sauntered to the register, pivoted and walked back. She laid the two tabs in front of Billy. "Pay up and get out," she said.

"If I promise he'll pay," he said in a little boy's voice, "can I stay?"

Ryan watched her, waiting for the look that said call the cops. Instead, B.B. marched to the walk-in and brought out a case of beer. By the time the cops arrived the other man would be long gone. She'd stock the beer and get home early for a change.

Billy lifted his drink and drifted over to the jukebox. Slowly turning the pages of selections, he looked back, checking the door. The place was empty. Scaggs had had plenty of time to score some dope, if that's what he was doing. The crew cut in the golf shirt didn't look much like the dealer type, but Billy had seen stranger.

Ryan emptied ashtrays and sopped the tables. Down the length of the bar B.B. poured from her tip jar. She glanced up at him, then over at the few dollars and quarters spread out in front of her, smiled a sad smile and pinched her nose. Ryan smiled back, feeling his face flush.

"You got five minutes to pay," B.B. called to the man near the jukebox.

"What time do you close?" Billy looked around for a clock.

"Five minutes. We close in five minutes," B.B. said. "And tell your friend," she said, "I don't forget a face. In my line of work, you learn to remember a face. If I see his again, I'm calling the law. Unless you're covering his tab."

Billy took his stool at the bar, looked at the two tabs, then pulled money from his trousers. He counted and laid the bills on his check then folded Scaggs' and stuffed it in his shirt pocket. "You should'a been nice to me," he said.

Outside, Billy walked to the west end of the town square. The sky was smoky black, the slight July breeze like a hot breath. He lit a cigarette and stared up at the old brick buildings, the court house and abandoned department stores surrounding him. This had been Scaggs' idea. The heel of his shoe ground the cigarette butt into the sidewalk. He'd just come along for the ride. Now Scaggs' Mercury was nowhere in sight.

A Darlington Police car turned onto the square. Billy back-pedaled into the deep shadows. The provisions of parole prohibited their leaving North Carolina. When he saw Scaggs again, he would say, "Where's the insurance man?" then answer his own question: "At the parole hearing." That was an answer Scaggs wouldn't expect. That's what he would say if something had gone wrong and Scaggs got that spooky look in his eye. He'd say those words and Scaggs' thousand yard-stare would disappear and Scaggs would smile and become himself again. But Scaggs and the Mercury were gone.

Billy lit another cigarette, smoked and waited. Scaggs' idea had been to go to Myrtle Beach, not Darlington. His idea had been to chill.

Headlights. The Mercury. Billy stepped to the curb and raised his hand to catch the door handle, but the car glided past him without a sound, like a ghost ship, then veered right onto Exchange Street. Billy shuffled to the corner. The empty car sat parked under a streetlight. He had a bad feeling. Across from the streetlight stood the black figure of a man, rigid as a robot in the shadows. Billy pulled hard on his cigarette, glancing the street from end to end. Crossing, he saw that Scaggs was amped, every herky-jerky kink and hitch hotwired. Scaggs was a man on fire.

"C'mere," Scaggs said in a whisper, his narrow serpent eyes flaming. "This shit'll knock your socks off."

Billy followed him down the street to an alley and into the recessed entrance of The Ridgle Law Office. Scaggs held up the key to the Mercury and dredged the pocket of his slacks. He unrolled a plastic bag as thick as his thumb, opened it carefully and shoveled up the white powder with the key.

A jolting icy kick shot up into Billy's eye. Numbness raced along the side of his tongue and across his cheek. He swallowed hard. The taste of tin glazed the back of his throat.

"*Damn*," he whispered, pressing his palm to his burning nose. Scaggs dug him a second bump. When Billy pulled up from it, hot blood coiled through his chest and arms, rushing down to his fingers. As Scaggs served himself, Billy looked out at the new world. Everything, even the darkness, was bathed in lacquer.

Scaggs smiled like a small boy. But Billy could see the man's jaw muscles clench, then soften, then knot up again like a cottonmouth's.

"This shit makes me thirsty," he said.

They heard music from the jukebox inside. The front door was locked, but Scaggs could see the kid mopping, his shoulders swaying in time. He tapped on the window. The kid didn't hear.

Behind him, Billy stood at the curb, his body electrified. The hot breath of summer whispered at his ear. The towering buildings seemed to arch over him. Eyes looked down from up there; he could feel them. For an instant, he saw himself from a rooftop position, through a sniper's eye, and himself looking up into the unsteady crosshairs of the shooter's high-powered scope. He heard the breeze and the tumble of a paper cup half a block away. "Let's get on to the beach," he said. "The bars there are still open."

Scaggs knocked again, harder. He held up two bills, hundreds. "Yeah, but they don't serve what I'm craving," Scaggs said, smiling into the glass. Ryan was punching numbers at the jukebox. The kid looked back then moved cautiously toward the door.

"Where'd you get that money," Billy said. He wanted to either climb out of his skin or do another bump of that kick-ass cocaine. "You didn't waste that guy, did you?" Billy turned back, sensing those rooftop eyes, imagining a finger on the trigger, searching the roofline. A dank charred smell floated upon the hot breeze.

"Down payment," Scaggs whispered, waving his bar tab and the two hundred-dollar bills, nodding and smiling through the glass.

Ryan stood at arm's length from the door then reached to make sure it was locked. Scaggs tilted his face to the glass. "Wanna settle up, little buddy," he said, waving the tab and the money, nodding, giving the kid that happy good-old-boy grin. Ryan looked back into the small office where B.B. signed inventory sheets and balanced the money every night. Where she sat now with her head in her hands.

Coach sat in the dim kitchen light staring at the phone on the wall, directing his will upon it. But it didn't ring. His wife had instructed him not to call her at work. His repeated calls had done more harm than good. She could no longer endure the silence on his end when she told him the truth, she'd said, leaving her with no choice but to lie about when she'd be home. They'd agreed that she would phone just before locking up. They had also agreed that he wouldn't come to The Paradise Lounge night after night to drink and watch her every move. His job at the Lawn and Garden was at stake. It didn't pay much, but without it they'd lose the house. They had agreed that these things were bad for their marriage. They had agreed that these decisions had nothing to do with another man, or at least B.B. had agreed with herself about that.

Still she had not called. Tuesday night, July 4th, the slowest bar night of the year.

He lay in their bed, in the blackness, listening to the air conditioner shut off then kick in. When Coach closed his eyes, the film footage inside his head started up. He reached for the radio. But the pictures didn't go away. Flashing snapshots from that crowded night at The Paradise Lounge when he'd first seen the man B.B. denied sleeping with. Images from his last day as a high school History teacher, the day a punk urinated on the state football championship banner, wagged his finger and blew spit-laced curses into Coach's face. Footage of his fists pounding the kid. The judge at his sentencing.

B.B. saw Billy's knife at Ryan's throat, tears streaming down the boy's pale face.

Scaggs Newcomb was happy. "I got an idea!" he announced to the room. He snapped his fingers, tapped his toe and sang: "Party-time-is-any-time-and-any-time-is-party-time, so let's *parrrrrr-dy!*" Then he was not smiling. He looked at B.B. "Get your damn purse."

Scaggs rested a hand on B.B.'s shoulder while she switched off the overheads and shut the place down. The remaining red and blue neon beer signs cast a dim purple hue over everything. Scaggs led her back to the bar. "Get the phone," he said. Billy unplugged it. From the jukebox, Vince Gill sang *If You Ever Have Forever In Mind.*

Looking at B.B. but speaking to Billy, Scaggs said, "Now show the boy how to pour a drink. I'm gonna have myself some *top* shelf," he said in that singsong voice. His hand glided down B.B.'s hair. "Yes, sirree. I want the good stuff. Makers Mark." Billy lowered the switchblade to his side and led Ryan to the liquor shelves.

Scaggs opened B.B.'s purse and dumped its contents onto the bar. Her phone and a can of hairspray tumbled out. "Look at me," he whispered. B.B. closed her eyes. Scaggs smiled.

Ryan set down a glass in front of Scaggs. Billy drank from another.

"Lookee here," Scaggs said. He switched off B.B.'s phone then took the cap from the hair spray. B.B. held her eyes fixed on Ryan, whose pocked face was red and wet with tears. The tears wouldn't stop. She looked at him as if the cops had been called.

"Watch this," Scaggs said. He squeezed his fist into the back of B.B.'s thick, red hair. She shut her eyes. He pulled. She resisted. The delicate skin tightened across her high cheeks. "Look at me, sweetheart," he said.

Ryan felt the cool blade at his throat, saw Scaggs' hand slowly close around B.B.'s throat. Felt hot urine soak the front of his jeans.

Scaggs snaked his fingers through the back of her hair, then pulled slowly, forcing B.B.'s head back. He lifted the spray can. "Hell-ooo," he whispered. She closed her eyes. He knotted his fist, pulled harder. He looked from her to the hairspray, lifted it and pressed the nozzle until the air was so thick she couldn't breathe, soaking her hair. Then he abruptly released her. The mass of soggy matted hair descended slowly, thickly. Still, she wouldn't look at him. Not even in the mirror.

He felt inside his pocket and brought out the sandwich bag of cocaine and a cigarette lighter and laid them on the bar. "Looks like we got us a little fireball here," he said. He tossed back the bourbon. Then he held up the can of hair spray like a trophy.

"Hey, Billy," he said. "Independence Day. Calls for fireworks." Scaggs struck the lighter then pressed the spray nozzle. A single burst of flame shot across the bar. B.B.'s eyes filled with tears, but she did not look at him.

He lifted his finger from the can and lowered the lighter. He watched B.B., waited for her to speak or move. For her to look at him. Scaggs waited for her to beg.

Holding the can inches from the back of her soaked head, Scaggs again pressed the nozzle. His fingers formed a fist around the lighter. "Some people hate the smell of burning hair." He winked at Billy. "I don't happen to be one of them."

Scaggs brushed the plastic lighter against her cheek, its head between her lips. She felt his breath on her neck. His lips touched B.B.'s

110

ear. "*Swoooosh*," he whispered. Then to Billy, "Damn, I'm gettin' *hot*," he called, giving Billy that hard smile. Scaggs set down the hairspray. "I wanna a drink. Markers Mark. I wanna make-hers-mark," he said. "Get it?"

"Good liquor," Billy said. "Lick-her good," he said. "I get it."

Coach waited another thirty minutes before he dialed. He walked outside to the garage where he'd hidden a bottle in his toolbox then sat in his underwear at the pale kitchen table and drank. Now the bottle was empty and Coach found himself in the land of irreconcilables. Trapped inside his head and too drunk to leave the room, he could not sit there and he could not go. He had to find her, but the odds of his getting out of his own driveway were long ones. Just the sight of his old, battered Mustang at this time of night would guarantee blue lights—and jail time. A certain end to his dissolving marriage.

On the barstool between the two men, B.B. sat upright and motionless, arms at her side, her unblinking eyes fixed on the mirror. Scaggs ordered Ryan to line up the top shelf liquor and then to pour a full glass. And now he ordered the kid to drink. "Don't you want some of this sweet mama, kid?" Scaggs said. "Plenty to go round. Me and him's gonna watch you lose your cherry, ain't we, Bo?" Billy smiled. "Come on. Say it. This here's what you been stroking 'bout. This here is your cream-come-true." Ryan looked away, his chest rising and falling uncontrollably. "Now drink the goddamn whiskey," Scaggs ordered. The boy steadied the glass, but its scent turned his stomach before he could get it to his lips, and his first taste sent up a heaving convulsion. The two men laughed. Billy slid the boy's glass in front of B.B.

In the baby talk voice he'd spoken earlier Billy said, "Show your boy toy how it's done, darlin'." He lifted the glass, brought it to her lips. Scaggs dug his key into the bag of white power.

"Yeah," Scaggs said, holding up the small pyramid of coke before him. "Show the boy how you part those lips." He shut his eyes and brought the key to his nostril. "Show us that mouth." Billy tilted the glass slowly, his eyes raking her like searchlights.

When the coke exploded inside his brain, Scaggs' eyes squeezed shut.

"Oops," Billy said. Scaggs looked over. Brown liquor dripped from B.B.'s mouth and chin, soaked the front of her thin blouse. She had refused to drink. "It's a shame to waste good whiskey," Billy said.

"Have to make the best of it," Scaggs said. "Pour us another round," he said to the boy. The two men watched B.B.'s face as Scaggs' fingers traced the side of her wet throat, then slowly pressed down her neck and over her right breast.

"I wouldn't call that a waste of whiskey," Billy said, cupping her other breast. They exchanged a look, their ravenous eyes blazing with savage hunger.

Ryan looked away, over to the small wooden door beneath the cash register, behind which lay a revolver.

"Bartender!" Scaggs shouted. "We've made a *disss*—covery!" He slid the coke bag over to Billy, bowed grandly then ceremoniously stepped behind B.B. She sat stoically upright, arms limp at her side. Looking up into the mirror behind the bar, he lifted her breasts and danced behind her from side to side. Ryan saw her beaded tears. "I've beeeeen to the *MOUN*—tains!" he shouted in an evangelical voice. "This calls for a *drink-ah!*"

Ryan poured. The small wooden door was six, maybe seven steps. He would have to move like a cat. And he would have to shoot straight. But there was the matter of the lock. "One more," Scaggs demanded, nodding to B.B. He coiled his arm around her shoulder. She sat as impassively as a mannequin as the two men worked her breasts. Scaggs lifted her hand and slid the glass until it touched her fingers, then he pressed her yielding fingers around it.

Eyes closed, she lifted it, took half of it down.

"Your slip's showing," Scaggs said, looking at the white rim of coke on Billy's nostril. "You fag."

Billy wiped away the powder with the back of his hand then passed the bag and the car key to Scaggs. "Free at last, free at last!" Billy shouted. "Step round here, virgin boy! Come be my dance partner," he shouted to Ryan. The boy glanced back at the wooden door. "You and me, jailbait, we's gonna cut the rug." He held up the knife. Then he laughed so hard he had to dance a little shuffle.

Nick Granger taught algebra at the high school where he'd played blocking back the year Coach won the state championship. This wasn't the first time Coach had phoned him in the middle of the night, sometimes incoherent, other times when he just couldn't sleep. But never like this, desperate.

Nick felt for his trousers and shirt then walked barefoot through the steaming darkness out to his car.

The boy thought, Lock or no lock snatch it open, get your hand inside, aim, aim, you got to aim, pull until it won't shoot no more.

Billy shouted to Ryan. "Bartender, my new young Maytag!" He patted the barstool beside him. "Here! Come sit wich-ya' daddy." He reached for the bag of white powder.

"No. No more. That's enough," Scaggs said.

Suddenly, out of nowhere, Scaggs was all business.

The eyes of the two men met, the eyes of beasts.

"Later," Scaggs said. He smiled and slid Billy's drink in front of B.B.. The two men exchanged ghoulish smiles.

B.B. reached for the glass and brought it to her lips. Her hand was unsteady, and some of it spilled, but this time she didn't set down the glass until she'd taken it all down.

"Hey," Scaggs said. "She's my kind of girl."

"Mine too," Billy said.

Billy bent his face close and flicked the serpent-like tip of his tongue against her neck. Scaggs smiled as he watched Ryan. The boy's tears had started again. Then the tongues of both men flicked at her throat and inside her ears.

Ryan turned his back and covered his eyes.

"Another shot," B.B. said.

Hers was the only car in the lot. Nick Granger pulled in and parked beside it.

"I'll go in with you," Nick said. Coach hadn't spoken after thanking him for the ride.

"Not necessary," Coach said.

"Just to see that everything is okay."

Coach looked at him, his blue eyes so sad Nick had to look away. "I can promise you, son, that everything is not okay. Chances are she's someplace else, not here, which is a discovery I'd prefer to make by myself. Thanks for the ride."

Coach lumbered over to B.B.'s Honda and looked inside. Nick opened his car door, walked over to Coach. He tucked a folded white slip of paper into Coach's shirt pocket. "My number," he said. "You call me." He looked up into Coach's eyes and laid his hand on his shoulder. "Call me, you hear?"

Coach steadied himself against the trunk of his wife's car and lit a cigarette. He watched Nick's taillights disappear. If the cops drove by they'd arrest him for public drunkenness. He'd wait in her car. She'd have to come back for the car and he'd be waiting. He didn't know what he'd do when she returned. But he'd be waiting.

He smoked. The light from the red and blue neon beer signs inside The Paradise Lounge bled into a purple glow, like a fire just beyond the morning horizon. Coach lumbered across the parking lot.

Ryan lay on the storage room floor, his hands and feet tied with lamp cord, his mouth stuffed with yellow notebook paper, his eyes taped shut. Behind his dark lids he couldn't stop seeing what they'd done to B.B., first holding back her head and pouring bourbon over her mouth and down her blouse, then unbuttoning it, peeling down her bra. Pouring more liquor but holding her head up now, and their hands—the greedy hands of the two men. When they realized she had passed out, one stood behind her, holding her head as the other tilted the plastic bag and dumped cocaine down both her nostrils.

Instinct moved Coach's hand to the door. It was unlocked. He thought for a second about just going back to the car. But he didn't.

When Scaggs parked the Mercury behind the dark convenience store off South Main Street, he told Billy he had to take a piss. But Billy didn't think taking a piss required opening the trunk. He craned his head out the window. Scaggs held four one-gallon cans. "What are you doing?" Billy whispered.

"Shut the fuck up," Scaggs said. "This will take about as long as a good piss. Don't you fucking move." Then he stepped behind the air conditioning unit, through a narrow door and out of sight.

Billy hunkered down into the passenger seat of the Mercury and felt for the bag of coke beside him. His eyes scoured the rooftops for a sniper's clear line of fire.

Inside the dark convenience store, Scaggs studied the layout. Earlier, he and the man in the yellow golf shirt had carefully laid out the lines of toilet paper, making sure the trailers were thick enough to absorb the acetone so the convenience store would go up quickly. That was the whole idea, that it go up quickly.

"This shit is gonna show," Scaggs had said. "This is some amateur shit here."

"No problem," the man in the yellow shirt said.

"Maybe not for you," Scaggs said.

Then the man handed over the bag of cocaine. "I don't have no use for this," he said. "But I know what it's worth. Consider it incentive. It's yours—I stole it. Or had it stole. From this black guy who comes in here. I've called the cops on him a couple of times for dealing outside."

"You just keep making more and more sense," Scaggs said.

"Word is out that I stole that dope. My place gets torched. Who do you 'spose torched it? I don't have any dope, never been known to use it. Don't make sense, do it? I got an alibi, maybe the dealer's got an alibi. What do I care? Let the insurance man work it out after he writes me a check."

Now Scaggs stood alone in the dark store calculating through the haze of liquor and coke how to pour the acetone evenly. As he bent over to check the trailers he felt the drip from his nose.

Inside the Mercury, Billy cradled the plastic bag in his hand. How to get the white powder from down there up into his nose was no longer the issue. He brought the sandwich bag up to his face and hit it hard. Then he slid deeper into his seat, feeling a stabbing at his heart, hearing his own labored breathing, smelling the metallic coke bubbling from his pores. He thought now of the woman, how he'd drawn back his fist when her vomit covered the bar and she blacked out. To hell with her, he thought. To hell with the bitch.

Going back to the bar had been Scaggs' idea, not his. He'd wanted to drive on to Myrtle Beach, but Scaggs had left with the man in the yellow shirt, and for all he knew, Scaggs would have left him stranded if he hadn't been standing at the street when the Mercury rounded the corner. And now Scaggs had left him alone with enough coke to send him away for a long time, maybe even longer if the woman I.D.'d them, or worse yet if she overdosed and the kid talked. Even worse if that thousand-yard stare got into Scaggs' eyes and he'd wasted the man in the yellow shirt, which he probably had since there was no way Scaggs could've gotten his hands on the money to buy that much coke. Maybe Scaggs had run off with the man in the yellow shirt, leaving him with the Mercury and the cocaine and the woman's vomit on his shirt.

Then Billy thought of Scaggs and the four gallons of acetone and his Lincoln in New Orleans and how the car had gone up. Scaggs had told him to stay put. Stay put, he'd said. Sit still. Like a man in the cross hairs. Billy felt the burning in his nose and remember the stench of the Lincoln's flaming tires.

Something electric flashed through him. He couldn't stay inside that car another second. No question. The Mercury was about to blow.

From blocks away Nick saw the whirling blue lights. Darlington cops and EMS swarmed the lot outside The Paradise Lounge. Inside B.B. still lay on a stretcher, her hair matted with hairspray and vomit. A white shadow of coke rimmed her nostrils. Nick saw that Coach had missed a button when he did up her blouse. He had called 911 then Nick. Now that her stomach was empty, the EMS guys said she would be okay. Nick spoke to her and she seemed to know him. He stepped back and watched a cop scoop up small samples of powder from the bar. Then the detective placed a hand on his shoulder. Where was Coach, he asked. Nobody thought to ask about the kid. Nobody noticed the small wooden door below the register. The one that swung open.

Scaggs divided his steps and set the gallon cans equidistant so that he would know how to pour. He checked the lamp cord the man in the yellow shirt had skinned earlier and felt to make sure it was plugged in tightly and that the raw wire rested in the plastic ashtray he would fill with acetone. All he had to do was pour and then hit the switch beside the front door on his way out.

In twenty minutes he and Billy would be on I-95. Twenty minutes more and they'd be off I-95, and an hour later they'd be in Myrtle Beach for breakfast. He walked quickly, sloshing as he poured. Choking petrol fumes filled the place and burned his eyes.

Scaggs stood in the dark holding the empty cans when he thought he heard something. He looked up at the front window. A sign there said "Fresh fish" and for a second the words struck him as funny, and he almost laughed aloud. Where's the insurance man? Billy would ask over scrambled eggs. Eating fried fish, he would answer. Scaggs opened the front door, set the cans outside, then reached back for the light switch. He heard a man's voice in the back of the store. Cops, he thought.

The explosion lifted Scaggs' body, flinging his heels high, plowing him face-first across the asphalt. A piercing hiss shot though his ear like a red hot needle. The back of his shirt felt like crepe paper. He smelled the odor of burnt hair.

As the flames sucked the night air past him, he staggered back to the Mercury. The passenger door was open. He pushed it shut. Blisters swelled his fingertips. He fell into the car and reached for his keys.

The howling flames sired an angry wind that grew upon itself. Scaggs stomped the accelerator. Yet even above the roar of the fire's wooshing thunder and the squalling, smoking tires, Scaggs could hear them—the last of Billy's screams from inside.

Coach sat in the passenger seat of the Honda, the revolver resting in his lap, his eyes fixed on the out yonder. Ryan drove. They had taken Highway 52 the seven miles to I-95 looking for two men, any two white men walking or riding, and now, having seen no one, they were on their way back into Darlington. Coach asked of course. Ryan told Coach about the hairspray and the lighter. He hadn't told him about the two men pawing B.B., about their mouths on her. He didn't have to. Coach had found her, half naked, her face on the bar. Ryan was ashamed that she had seen him cry, and ashamed now that he couldn't hold back the tears. But even his shame wouldn't stop him from crying again tomorrow when he told it all to the cops.

B.B. half-naked, Coach thought, nearly unconscious when he lifted her face. "*Who are you?*" she'd said to him, her eyes wild and frightened, her small hand fluttering like a broken wing above her face.

And his first thought had been to reach for a drink.

He and the boy saw the flames and the fire trucks' flashing red lights.

"Cashua Ferry Road," Coach said.

The last thing Scaggs remembered clearly was that floating feeling of the Mercury at 120 miles an hour on the straight stretch of Seven Bridges Road near the interstate. He'd glanced down for the bag of coke. Now he was lying in a ditch as wide and deep as a canal somewhere in Darlington County with the worst sunburn he'd ever known on his back and neck, a bloody face, and a left foot that pointed like a hoof in the wrong direction.

The road was narrow and dark, the turns manageable if you knew where they were, then long and straight for three miles to the Pee Dee River. Ryan took the curves cautiously, looking for a car in the deep ravines or two men ahead on the shoulder of the road, but coming out of each turn he pressed hard on the accelerator. They were nearing the long straightaway. He looked over at Coach. There was something he had to say.

"When we find them, are you going to shoot them?"

117

"You'll stop the car and get out."

"No," Ryan said.

"You'll do as I say."

"No, and if they are walking, I'm running over both the sons of bitches. You try to stop me and we'll die too. Swear to God, Coach. Swear to God."

Coach looked over at the kid. In his years of teaching and coaching he'd seen a thousand faces like this one.

Up the long straight stretch, a faint red glow of taillights. The Mercury, its nose pointed down into the deep ditch that emptied into the swamp.

Some fifty yards from the car, Scaggs lay coiled in the stinking shallow water beneath a gnarly canopy of kudzu, scrub and briers like barbed wire. He heard the car stop at the Mercury and the faint voices, two of them. Wiping from his face the sweat and blood that wouldn't stop, he shut his eyes to make out what the two men were saying, but the sound of the throbbing in his ears muffled their voices. He'd lie still then push on when the voices were no more.

As the car overhead crept near, the driver touched the pedal. Shrill metal-upon-metal. Bad brakes. A man's voice, "Car's empty." Then footsteps in the gravel.

The pistol hanging loosely at his side, Coach studied the spaces between the long rows of cotton and soybeans, watched the tree line for any movement. Half-naked, he thought, face down in liquor and vomit. "We'll catch 'em," Ryan said, swinging open the passenger door.

Ryan spun onto the pavement. As they neared the end of Seven Bridges Road, blue lights suddenly appeared. Coach gripped the revolver in his lap.

"Easy now," Coach said.

The trooper had one hand on his pistol and a flashlight on them by the time they reached the stop sign. Ryan produced his license.

"Where you headed?" the trooper said. He held the bright light on the side of Coach's face.

"Fishing," Ryan said. "Garden City Pier." The trooper aimed the light in Ryan's eyes, studied them. "The spots are running," Ryan said.

"Not this time of year," the trooper said.

He turned the light away. "Me and my Dad, we're going fishing," Ryan said. The patrolman pointed the flashlight at their feet and then into the backseat. The revolver was tucked under Coach's loose shirt.

"I need for you both to step out of the vehicle."

"There's a car in the swamp, maybe two miles back, North Carolina tags," the boy said. "A Mercury." The cop turned to look then handed over Ryan's license.

The cruiser lifted a cloud of dirt and gravel and skidded off, blue lights flashing.

The mush of grey clay bubbled between Scaggs' fingers, and hot stagnant green slime oozed over his belly and crept up his thighs. He heard something. He stopped. He lifted his nose as if to catch a scent. He held his breath to calm his heart and hush the pounding in his ears. The sound was closer, a rush of wind. Above him, flashing blue lights streaked by, and he smiled because now he was a safe distance from the Mercury, in this deep muddy ditch where even the dogs couldn't smell. He pushed on.

Blood and sweat burned Scaggs' right eye. But he stopped thinking about that each time he tried to tunnel through the tangled brush of the steep bank. He'd lift his left leg, but the foot kept coming down in the wrong place, sending a wincing flash of pain up to his groin. Still, two cars had stopped at the Mercury, and soon others would too.

He didn't know how much ground he'd covered, crawling in the deep mesh of brush and muck, how much space he'd put between himself and the Mercury, and he didn't know where the deep, black ditch ended. But he was headed in the right direction. This water emptied into deeper water. When the sun got up, he'd be near the river.

Scaggs pushed on until he could hardly move, his arms and belly raw from briars and jagged stobs, blood clinging to his face like fingers, his throbbing foot no more than a flipper. His neck and back were covered in scales of thick blisters. He stopped. From somewhere came a hiss like a distant voice upon the wind. A smell he couldn't name surrounded him. The night was black and still, silent save his labored breathing. He whispered, "I got one for you, Billy." Scaggs' bloody face morphed into a vile mockery of his Howdy Doody pose, yellow teeth like a clown mask. "Where's the insurance man?" he asked.

And in that moment, his enormous eyes wide and wild, the answer arrived in the fire and fury of his gaping, breathless screams. Churning upon him like flames or eddies, their white hot fangs sharp and fast as lightning bolts, the nest of cottonmouths, some of them almost babes, converged upon him, scoring his burnt and bleeding flesh.

Then the land was quiet and still. And although his eyes

remained expansive in perpetual wonder, serenity rushed in. And the steamy July night paused to listen, then took it all in, like a final slow in-suck of air.

The car smelled of sweat and vaguely of urine. "What now?" Ryan said, meaning the two men. Coach looked away. He didn't answer. The boy drove on. The lights of Darlington hovered above the tree line.

Again Ryan felt it coming up, that nauseous fear. He stared ahead thinking he might by force of will conjure the presence of the two men, certain that he had summoned the courage to kill them. The killing thing that lived in men was a part of him now, for their killing was the only thing that could make him whole again. The boy forced his shoulders up hard and straight against the car seat. His eager eyes awaited the arrival of the two, their faces branded into his memory.

But nothing in his headlights looked familiar, not the tattered billboards or the hazy, dim street lights, not the old black man on his bicycle or the headstone carver's shack. He felt his young body slowly seeping into exhausted collapse, the taste of bile in his mouth. He was only sixteen. This morning he had been a boy.

Coach faced the window saying nothing, seeing nothing. Then lifting his eyes, he looked into his reflection, brought up his hand, covered his face.

"Because of me—." Ryan couldn't breathe. "Oh, God knows, Coach," he choked out the words like a stutter. "I feel. All tore up." The kid couldn't look at him. Coach didn't turn from the window, didn't answer. The boy felt the tears start but he fought them back then spoke in a whisper. "I saw it coming," the boy said without crying. "I saw it coming, Coach, and—I didn't do nothing. Nothing. Me, Coach. That is me." Coach couldn't look at the kid. "I should have done something. If—." Ryan fought it back, hugged up to the steering wheel, and drew a deep breath to steady himself. "When you see her." His voice was steady now, clear, even. "Please ask her to forgive me. Could you do that? I can't tell her...enough. Will you please just do that for me, Coach? I don't know if I can ever bear to look at her again. I'm so ashamed."

Coach turned his face so the kid wouldn't see that he was crying like an old man. All he had for holding back wasn't enough and he was crying in that way that makes it nearly impossible to speak. "Yes," Coach whispered.

Ryan lifted his hand, rested it on Coach's shoulder. He felt the deep crying inside the other man's body.

"Do you think B.B. will ever forgive me?" the kid said.

Coach turned and looked into the kid's eyes, his own face bathed in tears. "Yes," he said. "Yes. I know she will."

Joe and Molly

Putting Harrison's iguana in the freezer was a big mistake. Or maybe finding it in a Tupperware container is what set off my wife. If I'd preserved Spike in Saran Wrap maybe Molly would have come to her frightening discovery in an unfolding series of logical deductions. Something like this: "No, that's not a piece of fish; Maybe—no—not smoked sausage either; I wonder if it's that pork tenderloin I've buried in here somewhere. Why, no. It's Harrison's iguana. Of course. What was I thinking?" But instead, Molly had cracked open the frozen plastic lid and taken in its contents all at once. Spike had died with his eyes open.

Spike belonged to our son. Harrison was eight. The only thing worse than not buying him a pet, I'd thought, was getting him a dog that would later bloody a bumper. A cat was out of the question. Molly's allergic.

Besides she already had Skippy, the Hollywood Chihuahua that came with our marriage. Skippy, she said, was far too high-strung to accept another dog in the house. She was right. The week after Harrison was born, Skippy sulked and refused to eat. He was the alpha male of the house, an attitude indulged by my wife.

Harrison is a gentle, quiet boy. He complains rarely, never demands. But he deserved a pet. I bought a fish tank and your basic start up variety of die-on-contact guppies.

The blue light of the aquarium reflected off his face as he regarded the most recent armada of floaters. "Dad, if it don't eat or crap," Harrison said, "how can it be a pet?"

We converted the aquarium and purchased Spike.

It was coincidental that most of Skippy's photo shoots that summer were on Saturdays. My son and I sat on the sofa, Harrison nestled under my arm, and watched Braves baseball while Spike curled up in his lap. We were a family. We didn't exclude Molly, but the bond among the four of us just wasn't there.

"How'd it go?" I said to my wife. Andruw Jones tripled to put us ahead. Harrison and Spike and I exchanged high-fives.

"Great," Molly said. She wore that yellow skirt I like, and her eyes were bright green in the lamplight. Molly is still a knockout. Skippy was outfitted in a red cowboy hat with matching handkerchief around his neck and six-guns at his side. "There was an *agent* there, Joe? A *real* agent? From Atlanta?" She smiled down at Skippy, whose giant bug eyes always made me nervous. I'd heard stories about Chihuahuas as fractious as this one getting so wound up their eyeballs popped out. "We have an audition in Charlotte next week, don't we?" she said to the dog.

"For what?" I said, my eyes returning to the game.

"A hotdog commercial, one that's going national."

"Going national" was an expression Molly often used when she responded to newspaper reporters from Marion or Dillon or Latta, papers with a circulation you could count on two hands.

"Skippy will look cute in a hotdog bun," Harrison said, trying to join the conversation.

"Nobody's putting *my* baby in a hotdog bun," she said, nodding to reassure Skippy, who for the first time seemed to comprehend the final destination of dogs in buns. "We're going national," she said, exchanging smiles with the rat-faced K-9.

Skippy's career began ten years ago, soon after the Christmas pictures I'd taken. Molly gave me a camera as a gift, and I'd snapped a series of photos of Skippy the day she'd bought him. I was just learning about lenses, lighting and shutter speeds. I placed the docile, shivering pup in different settings for effect. "Oh, that's precious!" Molly said when she saw the shot of tiny Skippy in the teacup. That's the photo that catapulted him into local fame, the one that later earned him a spot as the dancing dog in Darlington's Southern 500 parade. It was my least favorite of the series, which included a shot of Skippy inching toward a giant mousetrap, one of him swimming in the toilet (I included my hand on the lever in the shot) and one of him standing in a saucer of water sniffing an open electrical socket. My favorite, the one that resulted in Molly's temporarily postponing our engagement, was the one of Skippy in the blender. But it was Skippy in the teacup that made the papers.

And for most of the next decade, Skippy was a holiday staple, appearing in the local newspaper wearing a black and white pilgrim's cap and shouldering a musket at Thanksgiving, sporting a white beard and red cap at Christmas, decked out in a set of bat's wings for Halloween and holding miniature roses and wearing a tux for

Valentine's Day. We have an 8 X 10 glossy of Skippy with thick black sideburns and a guitar slung from his neck to celebrate January 8th, Elvis' birthday. Molly even gave Channel 11 in Florence permission to superimpose Skippy's face over President Clinton's on President's Day. In this part of South Carolina, that picture was so famous it ended up on Myrtle Beach T-shirts.

Harrison was away, spending the week fishing with my father, "the old man," a widower. Fishing is something they've done together since Harrison was five. I knew that if I told Molly Spike had died, she would toss the little fellow in the trash.

I'd like to say that Spike's death was more of a shock to me. But there had always been bad blood between Spike and Skippy, a kind of anti-multicultural, anti-diversity sentiment between the two of them. You could see it. And if Skippy was anything, he was an opportunist. More than once I'd come into Harrison's room and seen the two rivals going eye to eye. Literally. If you think about it, it's hard even for an iguana or a Betty Davis to compete with the eyes of a Chihuahua.

I didn't find any teeth marks on Spike. But when I lifted his remains from the aquarium, none other than Mr. Hollywood himself was right there, tail wagging, teeth shining, doing his little Fred Astaire number as he led the way to the kitchen.

The thought of telling Harrison sent me into a quandary. I wanted to spare him the heartache, which was impossible. In the end, I decided he needed the finality of seeing that Spike wasn't coming back. My plan was to preserve Spike in Tupperware for as long as necessary to help Harrison make the adjustment, but of course that plan went out the window when Molly unexpectedly discovered the plastic cryonics chamber.

Naturally I wanted to strike back at fate for taking Spike from Harrison, and from me, to tell you the truth. But fate is an elusive target. Skippy on the other hand—. Some days, while Molly was at work or out shopping, I'd take out my favorite photos of Skippy and pin them up where he'd see them. Skippy-in-the-blender went over his doggie bowl.

Harrison took the news without a tear, at least in front of Molly and me. He sucked in his lips and blinked at about a hundred RPMs, but he didn't shed a tear. Then without a word, he lowered his head and drifted back to his room.

We'd returned from Tee-Ball practice. I was carrying the canvas bat bag, Harrison his glove and a bag of baseballs. "What's that music?" Harrison said. The singing was so loud we heard it from the driveway. Molly, it appeared, was back from the Charlotte audition.

I want to be fair to Molly. She's my wife and I truly love her. I'd take the vows again tomorrow. She's still a beautiful woman, and her attachment to Skippy may have, in a way, been good for our marriage, though no question it brought hardship into our home. Molly is petite, short and blonde, with a cute little nose, and a knockout figure. I mean really. Molly is also an only child and probably the most striking genetic anomaly ever to come from Pageland, South Carolina, the watermelon capital of the South. Her family moved to Darlington, where Molly was crowned Miss Southern 500 while still in high school.

Talent scouts at the Miss South Carolina pageant swarmed to her after the bathing suit competition, and though she didn't place because she'd dropped her baton three times, she was offered auditions by talent and modeling agencies. She was too short and busty to model with her clothes on, and she's never been quick to get out of her clothes. Even now she prefers lights out.

Her undoing in all other categories was her beyond-repair-accent, thick and nasal, plus a rising inflection when she gets really nervous or upset? Soon there were no other offers, only me, Joe, arms open and a shoulder to cry on. Citing her impulsiveness and tendency to act on the rebound, her friends said she was marrying way below her station, which is partly true. She had loved another man. Some high school crush. Who, I don't know. She never told. I never asked.

In the past year Molly had been haunted by the uncanny success of another dog, one named Flatnose from Dovesville, not ten miles from where we live. Flatnose the Bulldog was famous for climbing trees and had even appeared on *The Johnny Carson Show*. Molly, who has an overdeveloped sense of competition, saw the same potential in Skippy, who could dance the fandango and shimmy with the best of them.

At the back door, Harrison placed his baseball glove on his head like a floppy hat and looked up at me. Barbara Streisand sang *A Star is Born* at the top of her lungs. It was impossible to talk above the power of Ms. Streisand's vocals or to compete with the birth of a star. From the kitchen we saw Molly on the sofa, both hands hovering near her mouth and a joyous trail of mascara webbing her cheeks. Skippy's tutu was pink and the tiny bra's tinsel shimmied as he held up his paws and did the boogie-woogie.

In the living room, Harrison sat in the recliner and began unlacing his rubber cleats. Molly lifted her head with a pleading smile, wiped the black tears from her cheeks and shut off the music. "We made it," she whispered. "We finally, finally made it." Harrison rose from the chair, gave Molly a little hug, and padded down to his room with his shoes in his hand.

When I walked in he was looking down into the empty aquarium. He turned and spoke matter-of-factly. "Things die," he said. "They're here, and then they aren't."

"Harrison," I said, holding both his shoulders, going down on a knee.

"No," he said. "It's okay, Dad. What I mean is that you were a boy like I am, I mean a long time ago. But now you're a grown-up. One day I won't be a boy. One day, the old man will be with Grandma." He looked back at the empty tank. "Maybe we can try again with fish," he said. "Maybe we'll have better luck."

I insisted that Harrison and I come along for the commercial shoot in Atlanta. I wanted to take him to a Braves game and I wanted him to see it from a box seat.

"Maybe not," Molly said. "You know how nervous Skippy gets when the four of us travel. He'll need to feel at ease for the shoot. He knows this is going national." I'm not sure what look I gave her, but with that look the discussion ended.

Two weeks later I packed the car. Molly has always had a knack for finding advantage in most any given situation. Years of sizing up pageant competition heightened her senses and refined her skills. We were near Augusta when she launched the question from the backseat where she held Skippy.

"No," I said. "Harrison and I are not taking Skippy to the game with us. Period."

"Please," Molly said.

"No."

"Look," she said, holding up a handful of pages.

"No. I'm driving."

"This place," Molly said, fanning the pages, "is called Pet Paradise, and this one is only a few blocks from our hotel. It's called K-99."

"Forget it," I said. "If you go shopping, you'll need to take the dog to make sure everything fits."

127

"Are you kidding?" she whispered. "Oh Joe, I want to *surprise* Skippy. Can you imagine how happy he'll be?"

Sometimes it's better just to keep your mouth shut. I had said all I had to say. My mind was set. Molly, having been a prom queen, misread my silence for weakness of resolve. She began massaging the back of my neck. "What are you thinking, Joe?" she purred.

"Right this second?" I said.

"Yes," she cooed.

"I was thinking puree."

Molly fell back, arms folded. The car was silent except for Skippy's snoring. You'd be astonished.

"If you think an iguana in the freezer has consequences," she hissed, "wait till you try to put a lizard in an icebox."

"It's okay, Dad," Harrison said. "I'll just tuck ol' Skippy into the pocket of my Braves jacket. We won't even know he's there."

We stood for the national anthem. Our seats were perfect, first base side, right behind the Braves dugout. Our hero, Greg Maddux, was on the mound. For the first three innings, my son had called it. Skippy lay nearly comatose in his jacket pocket. In the middle of the inning, Harrison looked down at him.

"Think he's okay, Dad?" he said.

"He's just sulking," I said.

"His eyes look sort of like Spike's before they started thawing out," Harrison said.

"Pay him no mind," I said.

We were playing the Mets and having a pretty good time, leading 4-0. I ordered hotdogs and sodas. With a man on second, Mike Piazza homered. Skippy began a slow, low growl that lasted until the Mets' catcher crossed the plate.

"That's our little man," Harrison said.

"He just wants your hot dog," I said.

As the next batter stepped up, I explained to Harrison that in a close contest the game changes with every pitch and that he should watch as the infielders made adjustments when the count favored Maddux or when it shifted to the hitter. When we looked down, Skippy had eaten half of Harrison's hotdog. For a split second I imagined gripping the dog's throat, his eyeballs firing off like foul balls and fans scrambling to catch them, the lucky two holding them up like tiny trophies. Instead, I ordered another hotdog which Harrison and I shared. Skippy grinned up at us as he chewed his.

When the Mets tied the game in the sixth, I ordered a lite beer for me and cotton candy for my son. They'd loaded the bases with two outs, and you-know-who was at the plate again. I drank between pitches. We both sat at the edge of our seats. When Piazza swung over an off-speed pitch for the third strike, Turner Field erupted. All 38,000 of us were on our feet. When I looked over to high-five Harrison, I saw that Skippy had buried his head inside the cone of cotton candy, which I suppose left the dog incredibly thirsty; because in the bottom of the inning after Chipper Jones unloaded the bases for us by skying one into deep center field, Skippy's head was nearly at the bottom of my plastic beer cup. We were again on our feet. But this time Skippy was dancing a jig in Harrison's pocket, slamming back and forth between the competing forces of sugar and alcohol. This time we all three were high-fiving.

Skippy did the wave with us.

I ordered another lite beer for myself and another soda and hotdog for Harrison. The three of us shared.

By the time Mark Wohlers came on in the top of the ninth to shut the door on the Mets, Skippy lay back staring up at the cloudless, blue sky, sporting a wide grin and a zeppelin of a belly.

"I think he just wanted an afternoon with the guys," Harrison said, as we walked back to our hotel.

When I opened the door to our room, Molly sat pensively on the edge of the bed, fingertips in her mouth.

"Thank God you're *back*?" she said. I looked at my watch.

"It's only four o'clock," I said.

"I know, but I worried every *second*?" She took the bloated Skippy and cradled him in her arms. He smiled up at her vacantly. A little knight-in-shining-armor outfit lay on the bed beside her. "He seems so – *calm*?"

"He knows he's going national," I said. Tears came to Molly's eyes. "Put on your swimsuit," I said to Harrison. "Let's go down to the pool."

The shoot was scheduled at the CNN complex, which was near our hotel. "You'll need money for a cab," I said to Molly. She was a nervous mess. Cab fare was all I had to offer. She didn't answer. I put a twenty on the nightstand. Skippy lay in her lap with his front and back legs spread wide, in a kind of do-me pose. I never knew Chihuahuas had so many teeth.

After an hour of Marco Polo in the pool, I was feeling my age. Harrison swam over to me.

"Think Mom's back, yet?"

"I doubt it. These things can take forever."

"Wanna play more Marco Polo?"

"Give me a minute," I said.

Harrison tossed his arm up on my shoulder. "Let's go upstairs and catch the highlights of the game and wait for Mom," he said.

On the elevator, he took my hand and looked up at me. "Thanks, Dad," he said.

A second after I opened the hotel room door, I pushed Harrison back into the hall. There was a commotion in the bathroom.

"Molly?" I said.

She didn't answer, but I recognized the crying. I opened the door. I can't describe the odor.

"I don't want you to see us like *this*?" she said.

"What happened?" I said.

"Don't *know*? Every time they brought out a *hot dog*?" She nodded toward the bathtub.

I couldn't see the dog, could only hear the irregular sounds of a high compression spray.

"I think he must be *allergic*?" Molly said. Then she boo-hooed. I stepped in to comfort her. The thought of confessing never entered my mind. She lifted her arm in protest. I stopped in my tracks. And there was the smell.

I got up three times during the night. Molly sat on the lid of the toilet, staring into nothing. There wasn't a thing I could do, no comfort I could offer, no cross I could bear that would bring her out of her sad trance.

As I stood at the bathroom door just before dawn, I'd swear that old Skippy blew the first six notes of *The Star Spangled Banner*.

Before leaving Atlanta, we stopped to buy a large plastic dishpan and a bag of kitty litter. Molly hadn't spoken.

"What's that sound?" Harrison said an hour later. Molly had fallen asleep.

"That's just Skippy being one of the guys," I said reaching for the radio.

When we got to Augusta, Harrison said, "I don't hear it anymore."

When we got to Darlington, Molly was still asleep.

130

Skippy was dead.

It didn't matter that the dog was as cold and rigid as a doorstop. Molly had to hear it from her vet, Doctor Hunter. I held Skippy at arm's length by his front legs and hosed him off. He looked like a Chihuahua on a magic carpet ride.

Molly said she needed a little time alone. She wasn't being ugly about it. So the three of us spent the weekend driving from Darlington to Charleston to Columbia. Harrison was in charge of the map and the list of taxidermists I had compiled. Skippy was in charge of the ice chest.

Whether it was the Forest Lake Taxidermist in Florence or the Wildlife Taxidermist in Camden, the story was the same. It was gently explained that Skippy couldn't be petted anymore, that we could look at him but he couldn't be petted. We were encouraged to think about the good times. Harrison and I exchanged soft smiles. We were told that if against the advice of the taxidermists we still wanted Skippy stuffed, the cost would be $500, provided that Skippy had not died of cancer, in which case the procedure couldn't be done because of damage to Skippy's hair.

We stopped in at the main library on the campus of the University of South Carolina to see what we could learn about pet cemeteries. The only place such things are taken very seriously, it seems, is Florida. As we were walking out to the car, I said, "Let's send your mom some flowers." She hadn't been answering the phone.

"Good idea," Harrison said.

Harrison and I spent Saturday night with the old man in Cheraw. Skippy spent the night on ice in the car. After lunch on Sunday, I watched the game while Dad and Harrison wet a hook. From the time Harrison was a tiny baby, the two shared an unexplainable connection. Dad had taught the boy to call him "the old man," and even Molly and I had taken it up. They came back two hours later with a nice string of fat bream.

I dialed again. Molly answered.

"Just do something with him," Molly said. She had cried out, her voice calm and steady. I explained what we'd learned, what appeared to be Skippy's options. There was a long pause, then tiny cracks in Molly's voice.

"Taxidermy is out," she said.

"He'd sort of still be around," I said. "And you've got so many of those cute little outfits. Harrison and I wouldn't mind, really." Now she was choking up.

"I love you, Joe," she said. "And Harrison. I love you both so much."

"Don't worry about the five hundred bucks," I said.

"No. You don't understand," Molly said. "The vet said there was cancer present. Just do what you think is right. I don't want to know, not for a long time. Just do what you think is right—for all of us."

"Dad," Harrison said. We were on our way home. "Do you know what an Oscar is?"

"An acting award," I said.

"No. I mean a fish called an Oscar. When I asked the old man if I could take a bream home and try him in Spike's aquarium, he said there's a fish that grows to about the same size called an Oscar."

Harrison and I stored Skippy in the bottom of the spare freezer, out in the garage. I suggested to Molly that she see a doctor about anti-depressants, but she refused. She really is a strong woman down deep. We make fun of those beauty contestant types, but it requires a little steel in your backbone to take the risks they take, to know, as they all do, that the day comes quickly when no matter what you once had going for you, you don't have it any more. The world spins faster for them than for us.

"I think I want to go to church," Molly said. We weren't what you'd call regulars.

The photos were Harrison's idea.

I took out the camera and the lenses. Harrison selected the outfits. Skippy had gone out like a sphinx, which limited our fashion choices—no tinseled bras to show off his shimmying, or puffy fandango pants. But his frozen pose was fine for the variety of angles it offered. I found ways of getting in his smile without really drawing attention to his bulbous eyes. Harrison, as it turns out, has a knack for lighting. We'd shot three rolls of film and cleaned the place up by the time Molly came home from Sunday services.

"The pictures will make a nice Christmas present," Harrison said. We were on our way to pick up fried chicken.

"Christmas might be too soon," I said. "Maybe Easter."

The Oscar was Molly's idea.

The next Sunday, after we'd changed back into our everyday clothes, Molly said, "When the mall opens, let's go pet shopping." As

132

soon as we walked in, Harrison and I started over to the puppy cages, but Molly stopped at the counter. "I'm looking for a fish, an Oscar," she said.

The cremation was my idea.

None of the funeral homes would do it. But the wife of another engineer where I work does ceramics. Turns out we're all big Braves fans. I didn't tell Molly of course. And I didn't tell Harrison. He never asked. But somehow he knew.

We began a family tradition, pizza after church.

"You missed my allowance last week, Dad," my son said. I was standing in line to pay while Molly waited in the car. "If you don't mind, I'd like this week's too," he said. I handed over the six bucks. "I'm going to the bathroom," he said. "I'll meet you in the car."

On the drive home, I saw the glass container of crushed red pepper in the pocket of his Braves jacket.

That night, Molly and I were having a beer. We have one on Sunday nights before bed. We were having this one at the kitchen table. She looked over at a spot beside the refrigerator.

"Thanks," she said, "for putting away everything." She meant Skippy's bed and toys. I didn't say anything. "It was very thoughtful of you," she said. Then she leaned forward and gave me a kiss on the lips. "Let's tell Harrison goodnight."

He lay in the blue light of the aquarium. We both kissed him then headed for the door. "Wait," he said. When we turned, he was holding the glass container from the pizza place. Its contents were a smoky brown color.

"What is that?" Molly said.

"Fish food," Harrison said, offering it to her.

She shook a little onto the water's surface. Oscar slowly turned and made his way up to feed, then circled down. Harrison lay in his bed beside us. Molly and I were on our knees, watching. The large fish rose a second time, consumed a morsel of the brown powder and slowly circled down again. Then it turned and glided almost motionlessly up to the glass, eye to eye with Molly, and gave her a slow, emphatic fish kiss. She turned to Harrison and then to me. In the soft blue light you could see the clinging tears.

"I think he likes me?" Molly said. She stroked Harrison's hand. "I think he really does."

Pete

The two red-faced Memphis cops alternated in the interrogation of Pete Hump. One would ask a question or two, look away to keep from busting out, then flee the room to compose himself. Whereupon the second cop would take over. Pete didn't find this Moobie-Doobie tag team act so amusing. After six hours of bad sleep in the city jail, he was still badly hung over. His head pulsed and his bowels churned.

The two cops hovered before him. "What's so damned funny?" he asked.

"How'd you get that face?" Officer Moobie said. "Foul play written all over it."

"Looks like it caught on fire and somebody put it out with a hammer," chimed Officer Doobie, his faux professional face a pre-cardiac red.

"One more time," his partner sighed, turning his back. "Let's go through this one more time." The cop's shoulders shimmy in stymied laughter.

"No," Pete said.

"You don't get a laxative until you talk."

"I'm not under arrest," Pete said. "Can I go now?"

"I don't know if you can go or not, pal." The cop stepped in. "You're the one asked for the laxative. Lucky you didn't choke on that key."

"Ha, ha," Pete said. "You clowns just crack me up."

Doobie gave Pete a gawking look then tilted his head to one side, like a bantam rooster studying abstract art. "What kinda haircut *is* that?" he said. "A Less-hawk? You know, the opposite of a MO-hawk?" The turnip-faced cop raised his hand as if halting traffic, drew his lips tight in an abortive effort to squelch his laughter, then blew a convulsive mist of spit. Howling, he lurched from the room. Moobie loped behind, leaving Pete alone.

Ten hours earlier when the Memphis police cruiser pulled up

beside his truck, Pete Hump's Plumbing #1, Pete's first thoughts had been of Russ Watts. Russ would take one look at Pete, his hands duct taped to the steering wheel—his head taped in the center where the airbag awaited—and ask the question: Where's Chloe?

When Pete answered with the truth, I don't know where she is, Russ would back the rear bumper of Pete Hump's Plumbing #2 into the front bumper of #1 with enough force to release the airbag and take off most of Pete's head. So when footsteps neared his window, Pete felt his bowels go all loose. Now he wished he *had* shit his pants. At least he'd have his truck key.

Doobie, the cop who'd discovered Pete, had apparently been taught to remove duct tape in the it-won't-hurt-if-I-snatch-it-off Band-Aid method. The back of his hands, one side of his face, and his left ear felt like someone had taken a belt sander to them. His face and ear were the over-ripe strawberry color of his hands, and the area just above his ear—a space the size of his palm—still throbbed with a bleeding sensation. But there was no blood in the divot where his hair used to be. While Pete's fingers gingerly explored the hairless trough above his ear, the door of the interrogation room opened yet again.

"What do you *call* that?" a new voice said. Pete looked up.

"Who are you?" Pete said.

The new cop wore a tan uniform.

"*That*," the cop said, lifting his hand to the side of his own head. "That's one funky haircut you got there, dude."

"Says who?" Pete said.

"Darlington, South Carolina. Sheriff's Department."

Doobie entered. He tilted his palm spilling what looked like two pieces of Chicklets chewing gum onto the table and left the room. Pete reached but the deputy's hand covered the laxative tablets.

"Not until we're done," he said.

Pete repeated what he'd told the Memphis cops about him and Chloe, about their running off together, first to Dollywood then to Graceland, about their having drinks at the Blue Suede Shoes Bar in Memphis last night, about Chloe's decision to choose freedom over love and his Jim Beam-inspired decision to swallow his truck key to keep her from leaving him. And about Chloe's husband, Russ, trailing them. He didn't mention Chloe's cracking his skull with the bourbon bottle. He said he'd passed out. And it was unnecessary to explain about Chloe's duct taping his hands and head to the steering wheel. Moobie and Doobie had squirmed like over-sexed junior high cheerleaders at that part of Pete's misfortune.

"Well let me tell you what *I* got," the sheriff's deputy said, raising fingers in enumeration. "I got a jealous husband who has disappeared. I got a cheating wife who has disappeared. I got the husband's ex-best friend with a Less-hawk and a truck key in his bowels."

Pete had no reply.

"And that's not all," the cop continued, losing count. "In Charleston, I've got a love nest with a broken-down door. And in Darlington I got a Smith & Wesson .357 and a big old knife with the wife's bodily fluids on it. *Plus* I got some of the wife's clothes in a shallow hole under a billboard off I-95. And guess what that billboard says?"

Pete scooped up the two tablets and began chewing.

"It says, 'Pete Hump's Heat Pumps.' That's what it says. Where are Mr. and Mrs. Watts, Pete?"

"I wish I knew," he said, swallowing hard. "I wish I knew."

A few hours later, Pete walked out of the Memphis police station holding his truck key and feeling like a featherweight. He hadn't been charged, since neither swallowing your truck key nor having your head and hands duct taped to a steering wheel by your former lover is a crime in Tennessee.

In the parking lot near Pete's truck the Darlington deputy rested against his unmarked cruiser, dredging his nails with a pocketknife. "Pete," he said, not looking up. "You could have saved yourself a whole lot of trouble." Pete kept walking. "You wanna hear something funny?" The cop stepped into Pete's path, stopping him cold.

"Not particularly," Pete said. "Comedy don't look like your line of work."

"Them airbags? They don't open unless the engine's running. Ain't that a hoot?"

Pete felt a hot churning in his gut. He stepped around the cop and kept walking. "When you get back to Darlington County," the cop shouted, "I'm gonna be on you like white on rice."

"That ain't funny," Pete said. "I heard that one before." Then he slammed his truck door and jammed the key into the ignition.

If there had been any place to go other than Darlington, Pete would have gone there. All along I-40, to I-26, to I-20, to I-95, he felt like an actor in a rewinding movie, like some force other than his own, some divining rod, was determining his course. He was returning to his hometown a man without a home. Without his ex-best friend, Russ, without the love of his life, Chloe, his best friend's wife.

Near Darlington, he lowered his eyes as he passed the Pete Hump's billboard, a man outside of time, outside of place, like a man without insides.

There was no chance of Chloe's returning. She'd felt the magic at Dollywood, taken the initiatory rites at Graceland. She was gone. Russ Watts could be anywhere, waiting to put a bullet through Pete's brain. His only hope now was that the certain end would come sooner rather than later, that Russ would finish what he had started, cleanly and swiftly.

In the house he had called home, Pete drank a beer as he showered and sipped a second one while he shaved. Then he lay on his bed staring at the ceiling, dust motes floating in the currents of yellow afternoon sunlight. "I'm a dead man," he said before closing his eyes.

He awoke an invisible man, to himself and, it seemed, to others. For a moment standing at the bathroom mirror, he experienced the distinct feeling of hovering above himself, looking down at the man inside his skin, the man at the mirror. He pulled down his Gamecocks baseball cap and reached for his keys.

At the Po Boy's Seafood drive-thru, Martha Ervin, who had taught him fifth grade, took his money and passed him the bag of fried fish and hushpuppies without speaking. And Tim Couch's sister, Robyn, the cashier at the IGA, looked right through him as she took his money for the six-pack and, without even offering it, crumpled the receipt in her hand then dropped it in the trash. Walking out to his truck, Pete Hump might as well have been a man without a face, a phantom.

He parked at Williamson football stadium and climbed its steep cement steps thinking of Russ and Chloe and then of Coach and B.B., theirs the love to which he had aspired. On the top row of bleachers he ate his fish and drank. "Just killing time," he said, looking into the end zone, downing the last swallow of his last beer.

When he entered The Paradise Lounge, Pete was sure Russ Watts would be there. Pete didn't want trouble. He just wanted to get it over with, to tell Russ he was sorry in a way that didn't sound pathetic, like he was begging for his life, like he was reminding Russ that he had once saved Russ' life. He preferred a bullet in the back to that. Because even though he had revived his best friend after the lightning strike, his affair with Chloe had sentenced Russ to a death worse than fate. Now Pete parked his truck outside The Paradise Lounge with only one purpose in mind—to get what was coming to him.

But Russ wasn't there.

He crossed the room for a table away from the bar and the jukebox. Nobody noticed him. Nobody pointed and said, That's Pete who ran off with his best friend's wife and tried to frame his friend for a murder that never occurred, who got himself beat up and duct taped to his steering wheel, who ruined three lives. Pete who shits truck keys.

Invisible Pete.

"What happened to your head and face, Pete?" Tami, the short-haired blonde waitress, wore red hot pants and a Hooters T-shirt turned inside out. Her pierced navel showed. "You look like you got caught in the middle of a cat fight."

"Hey," Pete said.

"Damn, that looks like it *hurts*," Tami said, leaning down for a closer look. "Plumbing accident?"

"I thought you were working at the Little Nashville," Pete said.

"So did I," she said, laying down a napkin. "Now I don't know where I'm at."

Pete took his first drink slowly, watching the door, waiting with calm, sad resolve for Russ. Suddenly he experienced a ghostly detachment, feeling at once both observer and participant, like a spirit floating over the scene. Like he was witnessing history unfold. Each time the door opened, he whispered the name of someone he'd known most all his life, this his way of saying goodbye: Evander Baker, Marion Walker, John Stuckey. George Miles recited Rudy Ray poetry at the bar. Robyn Couch smoked cigarettes and nodded approvingly while Marion Walker exalted Dale Earnhardt. A stranger in a turtleneck sat alone at the far end of the bar. This could have been yesterday, could be tomorrow at The Paradise Lounge. But it was neither.

As she delivered Pete's second drink, Tami sang along with Melissa Etheridge.

"Thanks," Pete said.

"You know this song, *Come To My Window*?" Tami said. "You have no idea how many times I've sung that song, Pete."

He studied the bottom of his glass. Tami fisted his wet napkins. He looked up at her.

"If you could have anything or anybody you wanted," Pete said, "what would it be?" She stopped, the wad held suspended for a second, then slowly and mechanically stuffed Pete's empty glass. Her face darkened and she seemed to gently wilt as if her insides slowly collapsed. She set down his fresh drink and looked up, away from Pete.

"I wish I could tell you, Pete. I really wish I could."

Pete watched her walk away. Then she stopped and turned. "I might say, 'Just to be the answer to somebody's dreams,'" she said. "But you wouldn't know what I mean."

He watched her cross to the end of the bar, to a man sitting alone. Pete felt a throbbing pulse at his temple. On the stool held by the guy in the turtleneck now sat the dark figure of another man, one more shadow than man. Tami laid her arm on the man's shoulder and whispered to him, moving her hand in soothing circles over his broad shoulders. He turned his face up to her and smiled. She kissed him lightly on the cheek then walked away.

It was Coach, hunkered over his drink like a man blowing to start a fire, a man reduced to his last match. Pete instinctively turned and looked for B.B., Coach's wife, the other bartender. She wasn't there.

For a long, long time, Coach and B.B. had been everybody's happiness. Then in one bloody minute, everything Coach lived for was gone: A surly kid who'd urinated on the state football championship banner, wagged his finger and sprayed spit in Coach's face. "Go to hell, you old cocksucker," the kid shouted.

"That's enough," Coach said.

"Fuck you *and* the whore you rode in on," he spat.

The jury saw the photographs of the kid's missing teeth. Now Coach worked at the Lawn and Garden to pay off the civil suit. His wife, who understood the value and power of her looks, had tended bar to save their house.

When Tami came around again, Pete whispered, "Where's B.B.?" Tami lifted Pete's glass, took a drink from it then set it down.

"You don't want to know," she said. "You really don't want to know." They both looked over at Coach. Tami again reached for Pete's glass, drank and set it down. "If I had words, I'd tell you," she said. Then she turned and walked away.

"Tami," Pete called, "I want to settle up."

"Don't we all," she said.

By the time Tami returned with his check, Pete had drained his bourbon. He couldn't stay. The room was emptying of air. He had nowhere to go but he had to get out. He stood and dug into his pocket.

"This early?" Tami said, looking down at her imaginary wristwatch. "Pete Hump's Heat Pumps?" She forced a smile and watched him count the bills. Pete tucked the money in her palm and pressed her fingers over it.

"Not anymore," he said.

"I know the feeling, Pete," she said. "I know the feeling."

Pete turned his eyes to the floor as he passed Coach, who sat with his back to him, praying into his drink.

"Son?" Coach said into his glass. Coach lifted one arm, draped it over an invisible shoulder. Pete stopped. Something akin to faith ran like common blood through this man and his team and through the citizens of this small town. And the heart that pumped that blood beat for his wife.

"Hey, Coach," Pete said softly, leaning toward the door.

"George," Coach said to the bartender, "bring my boy a drink. On me."

George, the team's wide receiver, looked over at Pete, then at the plate glass window where the hood of Coach's Mustang had crashed into the bar.

Coach patted the barstool beside him. Pete took it.

"How's it going, Coach?" he said in quiet reverence. Coach seemed to be considering Pete's question.

"You have to get that billboard down, son. Pete Hump's Heat Pumps? It's crude. Embarrassing."

George set the drink on the bar and gave Pete a pleading look.

"This one's on me," Coach said staring down into his glass.

"This one's on the house, Bo," George whispered to Pete, then turned and walked the length of the bar. Coach's guardian now, George Miles stood facing the window, arms folded across his chest like a chieftain or a pharaoh.

Across the room, Evander Baker stepped away from the jukebox as a slow Vince Gill song began to play.

"You know, son, the toughest part of the game—." Coach lifted his glass, held it suspended at his lips as he slowly blinked and searched for words— "is coming back from a loss. There was a time I could'a taught you that." He drank, then without spilling set the glass down softly.

The two men sat at the bar, heads bowed, through the first song, *When Love Finds You*. Then through the second, *If You Ever Have Forever In Mind*. Neither spoke. Coach's eyes looked like blue flames under water.

Pete drove the Old Charleston Highway. He wasn't in a hurry. He had no true destination. All he wanted was to say goodbye. But there was nobody to say goodbye to, only an empty Charleston apartment where he had made love to the only woman he'd ever loved.

Two hours later Pete shut off the engine outside the apartment and looked up. He didn't know that he'd parked in the space Russ had once occupied. Nor could he know that looking up at that small window and seeing in it the finality of love was what Russ had seen. There were so very many things Pete had no way of knowing. But he was certain he didn't want to go out of this life without one last look at the world he'd shared with Chloe.

The apartment door had been replaced, the lock changed. Pete walked back to his truck for the tools he'd need.

Inside, he saw that someone, the cops of course, had been through everything. The electricity had been disconnected. The sheets and pillowcases had been stripped from the bed, taken away in plastic bags, potential evidence in a murder that never occurred. He stood at the bedroom window and pulled open the blinds. Below, he saw Pete Hump's Plumbing #1, identical to Russ' #2. For an instant he thought he glimpsed the silhouette of someone behind the wheel looking back at him.

Pete lay on the mattress and brought a pillow to his face, inhaling the faint scent of what remained of Chloe, pressing his face into it, saying, "I'm sorry, Russ. I'm sorry." Then taking the pillow into his arms and whispering, "Oh, Chloe, Oh, Chloe," until sleep found him.

The distant echo of his own voice stirred Pete from his dream. He was neither awake nor asleep. "Swaying naked singers," he murmured. "Inside a giant canvas tent." The room smelled of brackish water and the scent of singed hair.

Pete parked on the Charleston Battery and sipped his coffee. The day was clear. He shaded his eyes and looked out at Fort Sumter. Either Russ was very near or, like Chloe, gone for good. Pete crushed his empty paper cup in his sore palm and dropped it into the trashcan. He couldn't stay in Charleston and he couldn't return to Darlington. And he couldn't sit still.

As he drove, Pete read aloud Charleston exit signs, "Mt. Pleasant, Isle of Palms, Whitehall Terrace," and for a time the sounds of the words and the images they inspired soothed him and led him north on coastal Highway 17. He drove slowly, stopping here to watch the Spanish moss sway in the woods, there to count white gulls on a weathered bridge railing. At Georgetown, he bought gas and fried chicken. In North Myrtle Beach he stopped for a beer. He pulled over and read historical markers. By the time he entered the city limits of Wilmington, North Carolina, Pete knew his destination, though he didn't know why or what he'd do when he reached it. In New Bern, he stopped for food and coffee, then stopped for coffee again in Little Washington to fend off sleep.

Lake Mattamuskeet, 50,000 acres of Hyde County, North Carolina, is famous for its goose hunting in the winter and its bass fishing in the summer, its origin a chance encounter of meteor and earth. Like love, its plentitude is matched only by its beauty and brutality. The land surrounding the lake, compared by some to the Mississippi Delta and by others to the Egyptian Nile, is so rich the soil will burn. Attempts over the past century to empty it for farming have been abandoned, for it keeps refilling itself despite all human effort and desire.

After high school graduation, while other kids were weaving across the centerline on their way to Myrtle Beach, Pete Hump and his best friend Russ Watts made a bass fishing pilgrimage to the lake. Teammates, they drank beer like men and swapped stories of cracked ribs and bloody noses from that championship season. Each thought he might become a coach like their common hero, and they laughed as they considered that one day they might face off in a fight to the finish.

The next day Russ was struck by lightning. Pete held his friend in his arms, pounded his heart, and, looking up into the sky, pleaded for his friend's life. From a blinding light above, there appeared a vision of paradise: a ragged carnival tent amid a vast empty field. As the broad canvas tent flaps opened before him, Pete ascended. Momentarily blinded by the darkness inside, he was overcome by the scent of sawdust and pine shavings. Then there appeared upon a candlelit stage a naked choir of heavy-breasted, thick-thighed peasant women swooning in ecstatic bliss. They sang *When Love Finds You.*

The two boys awoke, Russ in Pete's arms. "Watch 'em dance," Russ said. "In a tent. In a field," Pete echoed.

Now Pete was returning to Lake Mattamuskeet, driving through the dense, humid night to say goodbye to Russ Watts, wherever he was. For the life Pete had saved, he had more than taken.

He nursed the large coffee he'd bought in Little Washington, trusting it to keep him awake until he reached the lake. The two-lane blacktop, unerringly straight and endless in the headlights, divided miles of towering ripe corn. Passing through deafening crescendos of cicadas, Pete lowered his window and inhaled the rich black earth as he followed the headlights through this green tunnel of life. He couldn't see the lake's brackish water, but he could smell it. He was close.

Pete parked at the causeway where he and Russ had once camped and shut off the engine. At four-thirty in the morning there was no moon, only darkness and the smell of the prehistoric lake. Pete stripped, wiped his face with his shirt, folded it, and sat naked facing the water. The salty summer air was heavy and humid with life. Its smell yielded to taste, the taste of primordial life, of Chloe.

He drew his knees to his chest, rested his head on his arms, and closed his eyes. The quiet sound of the lapping water on his spirit was like a soft hand on his rounded back. He was his own meteor now, racing blindly through empty space.

The morning service began just before dawn, first with the erratic shuffle of living things: croaking, diving bullfrogs; the spontaneous burst of a screech owl; the occasional splash of a bass at breakfast; the long vowels of the mourning dove, followed by the full chorus of all things feathered. Warblers warbled and cedar waxwings sang in rhapsody as white cranes, osprey, and red-tailed hawks rode the high, invisible currents to their appointed stations. Slowly, Pete was lifted from sleep.

But before he woke fully, a weight descended upon him and he couldn't rise. He wanted to sleep, only to sleep. All around, life shouted to him to rise, but he could not. Finally, the warm reflection off the water came to rest like a tender hand upon his face, and when he opened his eyes, a blinding brilliance took his breath. Before him lay a glimmering path, a wide stretch of glitter, a celestial passage of the shimmering sunrise that lay upon the tide.

Pete was lifted to his feet. The water was soft and thick as warm molasses with the brine of first life. A gentle current summoned Pete, and he surrendered his naked, weightless body to the ancient water. He drifted out farther into the light that parted to surround him until the tide of light rose above his heart. Then farther still until his arms were lifted, free from his body, as if to say: I await. I surrender. And now he moved out even farther, arms open wide because he knew now that once he was eye-level with that path of light there would be nothing between him and the source of that light.

Looking up into the cloudless blue sky, Pete lay back his head. Water filled his ears. "I think this is it," he said to the blue morning sky, then raising his dripping head, he drew a deep, deep breath. He would go slowly and get it just right, find that place where light was all there was. Then maybe his heart could become like this lake, become one with it, so that this heart might recover from its emptying, might somehow refill itself despite all efforts of human sorrow and desire.

Dana

Dana held one hand under the sprayer head, testing and adjusting the warm water, her eyes fixed on the out yonder. She was thinking of her husband. She didn't know where he was or when he would come home. Or if he would ever return. On his way out he'd said what he always said, "Just a walk-through," but she knew better, and he knew that she knew. Every goodbye sounded like goodbye.

With soft brush in hand, she sometimes applied makeup for hours, averting distraction, timelessly drifting. But there was something about washing someone's hair, maybe the flow of warm water or the soft, wet hair between her fingers, something that made her feel connected to the person. And when she felt that human touch, silence sometimes became more than she could bear.

"Listen up, Coach. Here's the deal." His head lay back. Luminous beads arched as she slowly waved the sprayer head. "The phone rings, and like some bimbo I answer it and it's George Miles who somehow knows about us that one time, you and me, and he says please, please, it would mean so much, and suddenly I'm feeling like I don't have a choice in the matter. I hate that."

She set the sprayer aside and reached for the shampoo. "Sweet George Miles." Her terrier-like fingers worked his scalp. "He's the only memory from this rotten little hick town that I wouldn't flush—that I haven't already flushed." She rinsed and towel dried Coach's hair, applied a little mousse and reached for the blow dryer.

She glanced down at her hands. "I'm wearing a ring," she said over the blower's whine. "Surprise to this shithole of a town. Dana the skank—married to a man who loves me, Coach. To a man I love," she said over the blower. "I have my own past now, has nothing to do with this town or anybody in it. You're all history."

Dana shut off the dryer and crossed the room for what looked like a pink tackle box. She spoke into the box. "Just for the record, you didn't know shit about history to be a History teacher, or should I say you didn't *teach* shit about history, at least nothing that made sense at the time. Welcome to History 101, Coach."

She studied the kit, which was filled with brushes and small cylinders. Then turning, she lifted a CD in one hand and a small glass jar in the other. "Heard the latest from Jackie K and the Plastic Hearts?" she said. "My favorite cut is *Duuh, Does Rose Kennedy Own a Black Dress?*" She set down the CD. Speaking to the glass jar, she said, "Counteracts dehydration." Dana scooped her fingertips into the cream then warmed it in her palm. She thought of her husband. Of what he had done, of what could be done to him.

"You fuckers," she whispered to the room.

In short, quick light strokes, she dabbed the cream onto Coach's cheeks. "I was in your Monday morning class, Molly-the-pageant-queen and me. We both had the hots for you. You were too stupid to know it. This, I am reminding you, was *before* the, quote, love-of-your-life moved here from Hartsville." Her fingers glided along the line of his jaw. "So every Monday all hot and squirmy Molly and I swooned as you gave the class a recap of Friday night's football game, asserting your singular theory about history upon every play of the game. Every play ended with either They should have seen it coming or We should have seen it coming. You and these blue eyes." Dana stepped back to allow the oil-based cream to work. "Too bad you didn't hear your own lecture." She washed the cream from her hands.

"It's past time *you* learned a thing or two," she said over her shoulder, gently lifting and inspecting jars from her kit the way a bass fisherman will examine a top water lure. "Today's lesson could be about trust and fear. Could be recognition and respect. Or in this case endless regret. I remind you that I earned my Cosmologist's credentials at Florence-Darlington Technical College. So let's call this lesson The Cosmetics of Love." She unscrewed their tops and lined up the jars. "For starters, Coach, let's begin with the assumption that people come to learn something they *don't* know by picking up from something they *do* know. Love is consistent with your theory of history, which will be our starting point. You don't see love coming, but when it finds you, you say, 'Damn I should'a seen that coming.' True or false? Yes or no?" Dana ran her warm fingers over the contour of his face, up over his high cheekbones creating a warm, even, thin sheen.

"Cosmetics work, like love, starts from the inside out. Lust? Starts everywhere at once. Like the Big Bang. Fault of the manufacturer. So, just for the record, that day in your office—I'll remind you that was

148

before B.B. moved here from Hartsville—you didn't stand a chance, Coach. It was competition, something you know—mine and Molly's—and curiosity. And partly just the way I'm made. Every girl has fantasies about doing a teacher. I just happen to be the type who isn't satisfied with living in a fairytale world. You do remember Molly, right? The only girl in your class who squirmed and panted more than me? When I saw that she had the hots for you too, the whole thing became more about Molly and me than about you, not to shatter your fragile ego or anything. I'm speaking here about lust, Coach, and more specifically about the separation of body, that would be lust, and spirit, which is love. George Miles never called me a slut. Not even —. Never."

"My husband—," she said. Then, "I need a cigarette."

Dark Victorian houses lined West Broad Street. Only the lights inside The Darlington Florist Shoppe burned. She smoked as she crossed. The full moon was so bright it cast shadows. As she walked, Dana couldn't shake the feeling that she was being accompanied by someone from her past, a former faceless self.

In the bright moonlight she stood before the old Edwards House and read the historical marker. The house's architect, an officer under General Sherman, appealed to Sherman not to torch it. Dana lit another cigarette, tossed the burning match to the lawn. As she retraced her steps, she pictured Darlington on fire.

Her husband never said when or where or for how long. He was there and then he was gone. It was the only way, he said. And then one morning she would walk into the kitchen and he'd be standing there. He'd ask how she wanted her eggs.

Dana went directly to her cosmetics kit and began arranging her brushes according to thickness and length. She spoke with her back to Coach.

"I'm guessing you never told B.B., Coach. How the hell did George Miles know? Some people have a kind of ESP. They just *feel* things." Dana looked down at the lineup of brushes. "You know, don't you, that she might not—" she whispered. "Sometimes they don't come back. Ever."

She turned and faced Coach again. "Cosmetics work, like the work of love, has to support a greater vision. We're moving on to the next part of the lesson, I want you to know. The danger in both, of course, is over-application. When applied correctly—cosmetics and love—both produce beauty. They can make scars disappear, even. But when you pour 'em on too thick, they just make a mess, huh, Coach?"

"If you are a woman of a certain nature in a town like this one you learn what my husband calls 'projection,' which is when you imagine how you want it to play out, imagine how you want things to be: you see it coming so that you can believe it will come. A little girl's life is filled with projection. Prince Charming. Projection. Otherwise surprise, surprise. Stake through the heart. What you don't want. So that's what I'm doing now, Coach. I'm imagining how I want things to look. Considering what I have to work with and what I have to do. And when I have that picture in my head—the picture of the man you once were—I'll go to work."

Dana felt the air seeping from the room, an empty chill in its place. "Anyway, that's what my husband does. Him and me, we have a lot in common. I'm just doing a walk-through." Which was their code for the unknown, for what couldn't be said. Once, she had asked him about their starting over. "What can I do?" he said. "What you're saying, it would be like walking backwards to erase the past."

"You've got to give me a minute here, Coach."

Dana realized she was staring down at the flask in the bottom of her cosmetics kit.

Outside she drank. When she opened her eyes, the light around the moon glimmered like warm breath on a frozen cue ball. "I hate you, George Miles," she said, speaking up into the night, twisting on the cap. She heaved a deep breath and walked back inside.

"Vot ees the KIN-kiest ting vooo can *THINK* of ?" Vampire Dana said as she approached Coach. "Our VORK, as I have said, begins, MUST begin on the *IN*-side." Then speaking in her own voice, she said, "The history lesson continues." She worked quickly now, her brush strokes feather light, as graceful as the gentle flutter of butterfly wings. "I'm speaking of the cosmetics of love. Embalming fluid looks like Pepto Bismol. Erases that ash-gray hue. Works from the inside out. But let's begin with something you know, Coach, so we can move to something you don't know, today's lesson. First lesson in the cosmetics of love is cleansing—of the skin, of the soul. Exorcism in your case. Let's move on to foundation. In your case, foundation begins with what you're trying to cover up. Every love requires the proper foundation."

She set down the brush and jar then reached for another brush, another jar. "Last night at The Paradise Lounge, I talked to only two people. George Miles, of course. Sweet George Miles, bless his heart, I hate that son-of-a-bitch. And Billie Jean what's-her-name. Nobody else there recognized me, thank God. Funny how quickly people forget a slut, huh, Coach? But not George. He never called me that." Dana worked and talked quickly now. "*Everybody* was there. Well, not everybody, of course." She reached for another brush. "The place was as packed as race weekend, but quiet as a church. The jukebox was silent. Roomful of losers, you should have been there. I was digging in my purse for a dollar to play that song about friends in low places when Billie Jean spotted me. I saw the look on her face. She didn't remember my name. She didn't ask and I didn't say. Real pretty girl, dark. Very MYS-TER-I-OUS. Last night she was nice though, not all chummy. I hate chummy. Friggin' hate it. But she was, like, 'How you doin'? Are you happy?' You know, okay. Not chummy." She drew a deep breath and looked away. "Billie Jean's taking classes at Tech, where I learned the cosmetics of love. You'd be proud. She tried to lighten things up. Told me about a woman who wrote an essay in her English class? About when the woman's water broke in the IGA. I told her about an essay I wrote at Carl Sandburg College about why people ought to drink and drive. You'd have been proud. My thesis sentence was that it brings families together. She laughed and bought me a drink. Then when she saw the end of the conversation coming, she said, 'Nice to see you,' and walked back to that crowded, quiet bar."

For the first time, Dana looked at Coach's face. Really looked at him, spoke *to* him. "That's when George came over, which was the only reason I came back. He wore that sweet little boy smile, Coach, and sort of bowed at my table and said, 'Hey, Dana.' And I said, 'I'm here for information.' I already had pen and paper out. He told me what I needed to know. 'That all?' I said. 'Yes,' he said. He never even asked to sit down. I didn't realize he'd trailed me to the door until he spoke again. 'Thanks,' he said. Behind him, every silent face at the bar was staring all teary-eyed at me, even Billie Jean. The whole bar was one big teardrop. 'We appreciate it, Dana,' he said. 'Really. Everybody does.'"

"'Yeah,' I said. Then I shut the door behind me."

Dana rested her brush and opened her purse. She checked her phone, knowing that he'd never call. For her safety, he said. She went back to work.

"Love requires a foundation, but that is only the first step. In the world of cosmetology, we call what's next the blending of colors. The blending of colors actually lightens the foundation and restores the natural appearance. In love, this blending of colors adds depth—and shadows. It's your life with the other person, this blending. The foundation must be there before you have anything to work with—thus

151

the word 'foundation.' But the *art* of love comes with the blending of colors. The process is mysterious. It requires a sixth sense for texture, an eye for the elusive, a certain touch. It all comes from a feeling, and that feeling has its own home with an address it can't give out. This feeling, this mysterious act of delicate blending, it comes with serious risks, Coach. You don't want to make a mess of things. Unpredictable is what you don't want, that's what my husband says. 'It's a killer,' he says."

"I need some air."

This time when Dana returned from outside, she entered singing *Elvira*, an old song by The Oak Ridge Boys. She dropped the flask into her purse and washed her hands. She stood over Coach, but her eyes were out there, as if she were about to remember something. Or receive some message from far away.

After a time, she began. "This lesson can't mean much to you, this lesson on the cosmetics of love, if you don't understand the concept of application. If you ever loved your wife, I want you to take this lesson with you wherever you go. It is everything. You must answer the cosmetologist's questions about application: who, what, when, where. But you can never master the *art*, I'm talking about the art of love Coach, until you can look yourself in the mirror and answer the most important questions. How? And Why? That dash on your headstone between birth and death? That's your life. The How and the Why, Coach.

"You can't get those unanswered questions off your face. Which is why I'm here, you fuck, you. And George Miles, that son-of-a-bitch. He knows you can't, that's the reason he called me." She felt the tears welling up. "Cause I'm the only one who can remove those uncertainties from your face." Her words came out in choked, shuddered gasps. "You see, George—none of them—wants you to carry those questions to your grave." She looked away. "Oh, Coach. Oh, Coach. All that regret. They can't allow that. *They* can't take it. So thanks to you and George and every god damn redneck in this stinking town it's *my* burden now to carry." She gestured to the empty room. Her words came out like a flurry of profanity. "Do you understand what all of *them* are asking *me* to do?"

Dana dragged a metal folding chair beside the table where Coach lay. She slowly lowered her face and spoke into her hands. "With the right foundation and a perfect blending of colors," she whispered, "I'm gonna give them back the man you once were, Coach. For George and for every redneck at The Paradise Lounge. So that maybe my debt will finally be paid and I'll never have to set foot in Darlington County again." She looked over at him. "I don't need this. I want to be at home now. I want to be with somebody who loves me. Do you hear me? Not in a place where I never saw it coming, where I feel I might not see it coming *ever*. I don't want to be here, understand me. I don't want to be here."

I don't want to be here either, Coach said.

Dana felt the tears piling up.

Outside, she checked her phone. She smoked.

Back at work, she drew a slow, deep breath and spoke to the ceiling. "This is all you get, Coach, end of game, no trick plays, no chance for overtime. No hope for victory. No angel ever flew with a single wing. Do you hear me? Never. So they call me. And I am here. You and I. Now. This is me, Coach. Me, Dana the slut, who not only failed History but who couldn't even make her History teacher. Until now. I'm making you now, Coach. Reconstructing history. Last lesson in the cosmetics of love: Final Touches."

She held a small purple glass decanter trimmed in pewter and gold, shaped like a genie's bottle. "In high school, I wanted to be Elvira, the Vampire. Remember her, Coach? On the Atlanta Horror Movie channel? Black Latex and cleavage, and a screw-you-if-you-don't-like-it attitude. That was me. But the thing I wanted most, even when I was angriest at the world, was some magic dust. Like the Good Witch sprinkles over the girl, magic dust that erases her past and transports her to the world she loves, a world that loves her. Or pixie dust that allows you to fly away. Or maybe a kiss that brings the dead back to life." Dana held up the small purple decanter. Her voice fell to a whisper. "I have it here for you, Coach, in this old bottle. Magic dust. The only magic dust there is. This bottle is older than me, older than you. And inside are the finishing touches to the cosmetics of love."

She gently pressed the ball pump of the decanter, dusting his hairline and the surface of his face with the nearly invisible powder. "I met a man, Coach—." As she spoke, the hidden color underneath slowly began to rise. "He spread magic over me. He taught me the cosmetics of love. And I'm not sure where he is or if he's coming back to me, and all I have is this magic powder. For you, and maybe, one day, for him."

She walked to the door, the kit in one hand and her purse in the other. She switched off the light.

Outside, standing beneath the bright, full moon, she looked again at her phone, then felt in the purse for keys. Her soft fingertips rested upon something small and cool, something she had forgotten.

Dana opened the door and a bright tide of moonlight swept over Coach. Walking now in her own shadow, she held before her an offering, a small green plastic container no bigger than a locket. She stood at his side, looking down. She removed the tiny cap. Bowing into the bright moonlight, she raised the small container over his mouth and gently pressed. A tiny drop of liquid fell upon Coach's slightly parted lips.

Dana bent low, so close her lips were at his ear.

"It's called Sweet Breath," she whispered.

She touched a finger to his lips. "For kissing. For when B.B. comes home."

Vapor

"I can't tell you I love you enough," he said to his wife, the taste of blood in his mouth. This was Coach. He said it to her in the parking lot outside The Paradise Lounge. This was the Darlington 500 race weekend. Coach was drunk. He saw a man. He threw the first punch. Emptied the bar. "When a man loves a woman," he said to her, wiping the blood away.

I have a witness. Billie Jean was there. We had been Coach's students in high school. I was that faceless kid who sat beside someone like you. But a face empty of expression isn't the same as an empty heart. No self-pity here. Fact is, when you're a man without a face, you witness a lot that others miss. You become *Vapor*.

My mother didn't know I was watching.

My dad blew himself into tiny red specks lighting the gas grill he'd invented. I was a witness.

One thing I *didn't* see was the dead animal under the house in August here in Darlington when I was a kid. Could have been a dog. Big one. Maybe a fat possum. I never saw it. The dead thing was stewing under the kitchen. Outside, the temperature was 105 degrees. Our air conditioner quit. Inside, everybody's eyes watered. Except mine.

This was summer in the South. Power overloads. Air conditioners blowing like cheerleaders at spring break.

I'm not much with the social graces. My mother was right about that.

She said other things too, that I've never repeated. My mother had an affair with the air conditioning guy. She didn't think I'd see. She didn't think I'd tell. I'm not sure who removed the dead possum or whatever from under the house. But when the detective found the air conditioning guy buried under there a few weeks later, it was a cop, a big fat one with a face almost as expressionless as mine, who pulled the guy out. Stuffing the A/C guy into a body bag must have been like trying to put the Pillsbury biscuits back into the can. "He swole. He swole bad," the big cop kept saying as he sopped his face with a sweat rag. He hooked a rope to the trailer hitch of the Crime Unit's Jeep. When Mr. Temperature Control came flying from under the house, I thought of Santa's sleigh. It was between the arraignment and the trial, when my dad was out on bail, that the exploding gas grill event occurred.

I can't cry.

I drink bourbon. My dad drank bourbon. Coach drank bourbon. My mother drank gin. When I smell green pine needles or juniper, I always think of her. And about some of the things she said.

I miss my dad, the way he looked at me. We all miss Coach. And his wife, B.B.

Maybe crying is like liquor, opens us up in places. I mean after bawling your eyes out, everything's downhill, isn't it? Or is it up hill? I'm really inept sometimes. I'm a man without a face.

My mother thought I was stillborn. How would I know? You can't always trust an eyewitness. Which is one of the few things I remember hearing my father say. He left me nothing. There was nothing of him left.

This was South Carolina in the summer. Too hot to go outside. Heat stroke weather. Inside, the house smelled of the slowly expanding, gurgling dead thing under the house.

My mother insisted we go out for supper, to an all-you-can-eat place called The Iron Trough. The cool air in the Buick blew the smell of our clothes all around. I think that was before the air conditioner guy entered the picture. I'm sometimes easily confused.

We were standing in the buffet line at The Trough, and I said, "Dad, I'm hungry. Why are we moving so slow?"

"Never trust nobody," he said to me, looking at my mother.

"I'm hungry," I said. "We've been standing here a long time, Dad."

"They're all pigs," he said to my mother.

"*What?*" I said. I didn't understand. I just wanted to get my father's attention. I reached for his hand. "Dad," I said, "what's time to a *pig?*"

That was my first trip to a restaurant. Now I go to them all the time. I'm the guy in the turtleneck. *Vapor.* I was once a waiter. The best service is invisible. You look down and your wineglass is always full. But I had no social skills.

Vincent Howle. Bless his heart. Vincent sang "Amazing Grace" at Coach's funeral. Sang it beautifully, a heart-wrenching deeply felt rendition. Have you ever had a song inside your head that just goes on and on, and you may love that song, it may be your favorite song of all time, the song that was a hit when you-fell-in-love-wit-cha-baby? Music is feeling. It is. But the goddamn song won't stop playing inside your head, until it drives you nuts, I mean you love it but it won't stop spinning around, and you can't *express* that feeling because you're tone deaf and without social skills and your singing launches the neighborhood cats into shrieking heat-inspired porno mode. Now imagine every emotion you've ever had converging into one song, which is right this second scratching and gnawing to get out of your heart. Your face would look like this one.

Mr. Spring, our school psychologist, used to say I had a—quote—"rich interior life."

Spring is nothing like late August in Darlington. The smells I mean.

I didn't cry at my father's funeral. I couldn't. The air conditioning at the church must have been set to seven degrees. You could see your breath. My mother had a way of getting the last word. The flowers were few. I wore a suit and a cheap clip-on tie, a green one with red stripes. Now I wear turtlenecks. I wore a jacket, too, for my father's funeral. Still, I was freezing. My teeth wouldn't stop. I had the jitters.

I wasn't invited to help carry Coach's casket, but I did anyway. His feet. Although he never knew it, Coach and I were close. We went through a lot together. He didn't remember but I'd been his student in History class. I was the only person who didn't cry at his funeral. The other pallbearers had been teammates under Coach. Pete Hump and Russ Watts carried Coach's shoulders. George Miles and Nick Granger his knees. Pete and Russ were bawling. Walked with their heads down. On the way to the gravesite, I had to do that rudder thing to keep us on track. Nick and George walked straight and tall. Tears ran down Nick's cheeks like clear shoelaces, which I know isn't much of a way of saying it. It's the best I can do. George walked like a soldier, with the face of the famous New York Yankee who looks up into the stands and takes off his cap. Lou Gehrig.

I worked all night at the Darlington Flower Shoppe arranging the flowers for Coach's funeral. We're located half a block from the funeral home. Like the other pallbearers, I wore a boutonniere, a small white carnation. Before the service, people always comment on how lovely the flowers are. I mean at a funeral, who's gonna say, "Martha, look at those roses, I'd bet my vibrator those are day-olds."

A young woman named Dana prepared Coach. I was having a drink when George Miles, the bartender at The Paradise Lounge, called her. She traveled all the way from New Orleans to get him ready. "For Coach," he said. "Please come." Dana, George, and I had been his students.

From my shop window, I watched as she stepped outside to take a break from Coach. We walked together down to the old Edwards house, which was spared when Sherman marched through. Dana hates Darlington, she'd like to see the whole city burn. Small towns, like small children, can be especially cruel.

She smoked and talked to herself and cursed George Miles, who wasn't there, and to Coach, who was, but dead.

I have fears. But dying isn't one of them.

That sounds like tough guy talk. That's Clint Eastwood material. I was anything but a tough guy at Coach's funeral. Or Dad's. The good thing about a gas grill explosion is there's not much to cry over. Poof. But Coach was another matter. I waited at the end of the line of pallbearers as each placed the white carnation I'd prepared on Coach's casket.

Nick Granger said, "We love you, Coach." George Miles didn't speak. He just ran his hand up and down in a soothing motion over the shiny persimmon, slowly, back and forth. Pete and Russ were next. They were silent, just stood side by side looking down.

"I'm sorry, Russ," Pete said. "So, so sorry." Then he turned and hugged Russ and they both boo-hooed. Then Russ returned the embrace.

That left only me. I set my carnation on top on the wreath of white roses, closed my eyes and considered the years and all that I had seen. I searched for words.

"Watch'em dance," I said over his body. "Hear'em sing."

Coach and Vapor

It is the only light in the hospital room, a solitary column of soft dim light that falls over Coach's sleeping face. A mesh of tubes and wires connect what is left of him to the world. On the wall above the bed hang the high school football jerseys of George Miles, Pete Hump, Russ Watts, Nick and Dave Granger. A state championship football trophy sits on a small table. Beside the table, an autographed life-size cardboard cutout of Dale Earnhardt smiles down on Coach. At the foot of the bed George and Billy Jean stand shoulder to shoulder.

The door opens. An old nurse with the face of a man enters. "Time's up," she says. The nurse places a hand on Billy Jean, a hand on George. "He's deep in the woods, children," she says.

George jams his hands into his back pockets. Billy Jean rests her head against his chest.

"Time," the nurse says.

George fists away his tears. Billy Jean whispers into Coach's ear. She kisses his cheek.

His arms levitate. He whispers, "B.B.?"

Billy Jean can hardly speak. "No, Coach," she says. "Not B.B." She kisses his cheek a second time and his arms descend to rest at his side.

Billy Jean and George follow the old nurse out of the room.

From a dark corner, Vapor lifts a small wooden chair, steps into the grey light and sets the chair beside the bed.

Coach's eyes remain shut. "I smell roses," he says.

"Really?" Vapor says. "I stopped smelling them years ago. In my line of work—."

The old Nurse leads in Marion Walker, Evander Baker, and John Stuckey. Both Marion and Evander hold a white plaster of Paris square. Coach lies unconscious.

"You have five, maybe ten minutes," she says. "He's deep in the

159

woods."

Marion and Evander kneel into the darkness on either side of Coach. Each sets the white plaster square on the bed near Coach's hand.

"Evander and I made these for you," Marion whispers.

"We lifted them from the Walk of Fame in town," Evander chimes.

The white casts are hand print impressions. Marion takes Coach's right hand and aligns his fingers over the cast. "This is Earnhardt senior's," he says. Marion searches Coach's face for some sign of renewed life, finds none. "This is all I've got to give you, Coach. It's all I got."

Evander places the fingers of Coach's left hand over the other cast. "And just in case the Devil's doing the dealing," he says, "these here are Jeff Gordon."

John Stuckey, Marion Walker, and Evander bow in prayer. A voice behind them speaks softly. "It's time."

John Stuckey stands at bedside, presses Coach's palm to his chest. "Feel that, Coach? It's a faulty heart valve. Sounds like a tambourine every time I'm near a pretty woman. But it works, Coach. This heart. It still works."

Vapor again sets his chair beside Coach's bed.

Coach's eyes slowly open. "What's the deal with the turtleneck?"

"It's a long story."

"Who are you?"

"Vapor."

"Do I know you?"

"Yes."

"Well, hey." His eyes close. "Are you here to take me home?"

"No. Not me, Coach."

In the distance a ragged carnival tent sits in a vast, dusty, empty field. From inside, the faint sound of a church choir drifts upon the warm breeze. Coach stands at the tent's entrance. Its canvas door flaps separate and he enters.

Above the singing, Coach hears Vapor's voice at his ear. "Don't think too much about it."

"The choir?"

"Yes. Just watch 'em dance, Coach. Just hear 'em sing."

On an ancient wooden stage, three rows of small brown women

160

sway in rapture. Their naked bodies, like Gaugain's Tahitian nudes, are painted in bright earth shades. At the chorus of *When Love Finds You* their voices swell in ecstasy.

A little smile forms on his lips. "Yes," Coach whispers. "Yes. That's something, ain't it? That's really something. It is. The way they dance and sing."

Tim and Billie Jean

Her name was Billie Jean. And the moment she turned and their eyes met, something passed between him and Billie Jean, a feeling beyond words, and Tim's knees went all Gumby. He tipped his cap and offered his hand. "Glad to meet you, Billie Jean," he said. Tim asked if he could order Billie Jean a drink. She said yes. Time passed. He kept asking and she kept saying yes. Time passed into no time.

Five hours later when George Miles yelled Last Call at The Paradise Lounge, everybody was drunker than dogs.

"Hey, *George*," Tim called. He had to shout above the wailing crowd, their arms stitched across one another's shoulders, their faces tilted up like howlers, everybody dancing and singing *You Shook Me All Night Long* with AC/DC—everybody but Tim, who was trying before everything shut down to order a couple of shots for him and the dark beauty beside him. "Hey, *G-e-o-r-g-e*," he shouted again. George Miles, the bartender, had done that thing where he flipped his eyelids up, exposing their underside, and was air-humping a path behind the bar, working his arms and hands like an Egyptian, doing his air-humping-Egyptian-fish eye dance.

George smiled and lifted his hand to the tide of happy faces that filled The Paradise Lounge. "That's *something*, ain't it," George shouted to Tim. Even George was drunk.

Billie Jean, who was doing a John Philip Sousa marching-in-place routine, turned and gripped Tim's arm with both hands and began milking his muscle.

Behind the bar, George lifted one hand in a limp-wristed sort of way and pumped his pointer at Tim as he stutter stepped toward him, his lips all puckered like Jagger's, his eyelids peeled back. "Yeah, YOU!" he shouted with the music. His head hammered away like a woodpecker's.

Tim held up two fingers. "Fireballs," he shouted. George did a little spin move and humped back toward the register.

"No, not Fiiire-balls," Billie Jean said, marching to the music and tossing her hair like a pompom from side to side. "I'm drunker than a dog." The thumping, foot-slamming music was winding down, but Billie Jean was still climbing Tim's arm like a fireman's pole. She'd begun to do that air hump thing, too. Tim wrapped his arms around her and pulled Billie Jean tight against his chest. He felt his heart beating against her breast.

"One Fireball," he yelled to George then turned his eyes to the stunning black-haired sweet thing clinging to him. The music faded, but she kept up the humping pole dance, eyes shut tight in her bobblehead. "And one Fuzzy Nipple," Tim called out.

"Fuzzy Navel," Billie Jean corrected, eyes still closed. "Hairy Nipple."

The two looked like they were walking through an earthquake, *trying* to make it to somebody's car. When their shoulders collided, holding hands was the only thing that kept them from spinning off into infinity. It was a long walk. By the time they'd jitterbugged their way to Billie Jean's Mustang, she had to lay both palms on the hood and find her bearings before dredging her purse for keys.

In the shadow side of the small back seat, the two tumbled and swayed like passengers on a tilt-a-whirl. Their mouths kept sliding off one another's, and when Tim reached to hold Billie Jean's face steady he narrowly avoided jabbing a finger in her eye. To compensate, he attempted a Guinness record deep tongue kiss. After a time she exhaled mightily and their mouths made a farting sound. Somewhere in the mix and tumble, somebody's foot hit the door latch and the interior light came on.

"What are you doing?" Billie Jean said, only it sounded like a single vowel on a yo-yo. "Whhaaaa—r—yoooooo—DOOoooN?!" she said again. She knew exactly what Tim was doing. Trying without much luck to unbutton her blouse.

He looked down at his blurred, webbed fingers. Like trying to put a worm on a hook in a hurricane. At night, he thought.

"Whaaaaaa?" she said again, this time shoving him back with enough force to send the car door open. "Loo-cat-*mi*," she said. "Whaz my-name?"

Tim swallowed hard. He'd forgotten. Every ounce of hydraulic power left his manhood. He gave her that What? After-all-we-been-through? look.

She began re-buttoning his sorry work.

"Jelly Bean," he whispered.

He knew that was wrong, but it sounded so right.

She tilted her face to one side, puppy-head like. "That's so *sweet*," she said. Her eyes puddled. She drew a deep breath and looked away from him. "I been so looone-ly?" she whispered.

"Me, too," he said. "All my life."

She unfastened the first two buttons and pointed at her bra. "Unsnaps in the front," she said, reclining into the light.

She told him to close his eyes. "And keep 'em closed," she said. He kissed and nuzzled but with eyes shut his mouth kept sliding off her fine breast, missing its mark. "Don look, Don look," she said. So Tim opened his eyes wide. "No!" she snapped, gripping his ears like handlebars and forcing his face into her abundant chest. To steady himself Tim gently laid his hands on each of her ribs where his thumbs rested on identical moles.

A message written in electric Braille shot up his fingertips and a blinding whiteness flooded his brain. He swooned to an intimacy, a warmth.

"No!" Jelly Bean shouted again, pushing him away.

Now it was Tim who did the puppy head tilt. He looked upon her nakedness with adoring awe and wonder.

She turned her head and covered her eyes. "Poly-the-li-a is the fancy name for it," Jelly Bean said, looking out the window now and reaching to pull her shirt together. "I'm a freak."

"I don't care about a few freckles or moles," he whispered, moving in to get a better look.

She placed her bare foot in the center of his chest. "It ain't funny," she said, digging her toes in.

"I ain't laughing," he said sincerely, reaching to touch.

She pushed.

Tim spilled from the tilt-a-whirl.

Teetering on one knee outside the Mustang's door, he stretched his arms like wings to balance himself. When the earth stopped rolling, he slowly lifted his head. His breath slipped away.

Jelly Bean lay with her sad face turned from the soft light, her hand upon one bare breast. Tim thought she looked like a beautiful but sorrowful painting. Again he extended his hand to her. "I been thinking you were special since I laid eyes on you," he said almost without breath.

"I still do." He didn't know where his words came from. They'd formed in a place of their own, arrived effortlessly at his lips. She lifted her face to the light, her eyes mournful and wet.

"I just didn't know how to say it," Tim heard himself say, looking up as best he could into her eyes. "I want to tell you. But I don't have the words." Her eyes spilled over. Even drunk, Tim knew that love, when it was true, was one of life's mysteries, its undeserved and unexpected arrival more likely than not to blindside a man. There was no explaining and no need to. Misfortune had taught him that much.

She looked back at him and thumbed away the tears. "What's my name?" she said.

The night's silence rushed in and filled the space between them.

Eyes closed, Tim felt his hands float upward like a shaman's and his palms unite in an attitude of prayer. He lifted his eyes to hers.

"Billie Jean," he said, the words springing up from that magic place, and he thought, Thank you, God, thank you, God. These words not slurred at all.

www.ingramcontent.com/pod-product-compliance
Lightning Source LLC
Chambersburg PA
CBHW031238260626
47169CB00007B/2350